Gorgeous George

And the Jumbo Jobby Juicer

Or if you don't know what a jobby is…
Gorgeous George and the Pink Poo Power Pump

By
Stuart Reid

Illustrations and Cover
By John Pender

i

Gorgeous Garage Publishing Ltd
Falkirk, Scotland

www.stuart-reid.com

DEDICATION

For the help and advice of Keith (at Strident),
John's skills and Lisa the lawyer at the Society of
Authors for helping to break the chains.

And of course, to Audrey, Jess and Charley,
who now expect me to put their names in the
front of all my books.

Reading Rocks!

*For my wife Angela and my little boy Lucas.
Who's love, encouragement and unrelenting
patience means the absolute world me.*

*Thank you for letting daddy
live out his drawing dream!*

*Love always,
John xXx*

CONTENTS

Chapter 1 – The Circus Comes to Town

'Come on, lad,' shouted Grandpa Jock, 'We'll be late for the circus!'

Grandpa Jock was hopping back and forward from one foot to the other at the bottom of the stairs. His bagpipes were hanging over the end of the bannister and the mad old Scotsman jabbed at them a few times with an impatient volley of punches. The bagpipes groaned and wheezed their disgust.

'And don't forget your wellies!'

His grandson George hated wearing wellington boots; his socks always slipped down his feet, half on and half off. He rushed down the stairs, leapt the bottom three together and bounced back up. He slipped on his green rubber boots and searched around frantically for his jacket. 'What's the rush, Grandpa?'

'It's not just any old circus. It's Pippo and Zippy's Amazing Animal Circus!' yelled Grandpa Jock, waving his hands above his head, 'This is the last circus in Britain using real live animals. They've got lions and seals and elephants and they've even got monkeys trained like clowns and they're coming to our town. Here, today, to Little Pumpington.'

Grandpa Jock's ginger hair was sticking out at the sides more than usual; it always did this when he was excited or blowing extra hard on his bagpipes. His big purple nose was almost glowing as the old man worked himself into a frenzy of agitation and anticipation. George was slightly nervous since Grandpa Jock had been known to wee himself a little bit when he became over-excited. George pulled his grandpa by the arm and led him out of the back door, hoping he'd calm down now that they were heading towards the parade ground.

'Their last show, eh Grandpa?' George said calmly.

'The animals will be going off to good homes by the end of the week.'

'Which is all the more reason for us not to miss this parade, lad.' Grandpa Jock had clenched his fists tightly and was shaking them up and down. 'This is a real old-fashioned circus; a proper circus, not like these namby-pamby shows nowadays.'

'But isn't it a bit cruel to keep animals trapped in cages and forced to do tricks,' asked George, certain that the government's new rules on the proper treatment of animals was in the creatures' best interests.

'Nonsense, lad. Animals love doing tricks,' insisted the old Scotsman, 'I remember when I was a boy there was a dancing bear used to visit our village in the Highlands; jigged its wee heart out every year. Loved to dance, so it did. Until the last time, that is. Bit of a messy business with the bear's handler.'

'What happened, Grandpa?' George raised an eyebrow.

Grandpa Jock grimaced and sharply drew in air through his wobbly false teeth, 'Let's just say the man can only count up to seven using his fingers now.'

'Urgh gross, Grandpa!'

'Well, things were a bit different in my day.'

Trouble was no one knew when Grandpa Jock's day actually was, not even Grandpa Jock. He'd stopped counting his birthdays about forty years ago and usually just made up any age that suited him. It was rumoured that he could be anywhere between seventy-two and ninety-eight.

'We didn't have television or anything like that, boy,' lectured the old fellow, 'We needed live entertaining. And if the bear didn't want to dance, the man would poke it with his stick. I think the bear just got fed up with it in the end.'

'That's why it's wrong to lock animals up, Grandpa,' shrugged George.

'Aye, lad but there's no finer spectacle than seeing a parade of elephants marching past, blowing their trumpets and feeling the ground shake as they stomp by.' Grandpa Jock started to clump his wellington boots up and down on the pavement, waving his arm around the front of his face like a trunk.

'And we should stop for peanuts and buns to feed them!' Grandpa Jock's eyes ablaze with excitement.

George shook his head. 'You can't feed animals those kinds of foods, Grandpa. They need special diets.' As much as his Grandpa Jock was great fun, he did get carried away at times so George decided to pick up the pace, suggesting they might be late and hoping his grandpa would forget about illegally feeding animals.

Grandpa Jock skipped a couple of steps to keep up, his stiff old legs snapping together as if pulled by invisible elastic bands. As George glanced to the side to check his grandpa was still there, he didn't notice what he'd stepped in; he just felt his foot slide forward on something mushy and black.

Scccchhhhcoooooooooooot!

'Urggggh, what was that, Grandpa?' exclaimed George as he regained his balance. He looked down to see a gooey brown trail of ooze smeared across the pavement. Grandpa Jock's shoulders were bouncing up and down. He pushed his hand across his mouth to stop his false teeth from falling out as he giggled uncontrollably.

'It's not funny, Grandpa,' complained George, leaning against the wall and inspecting the sole of his shoe. Luckily it was not gummed up with anything unpleasant. The old man was still chuckling.

'I thought that only happened in cartoons,' smirked Grandpa Jock. 'You slipped on a banana skin, lad.'

George looked closer at the black mushy streak on the

concrete slabs. To George's relief, the lump at the front, although dark and squidgy, was almost recognisable as a banana skin and the brown gooey smear was the remnants of a very old, very mushy banana. It had been whole but the pressure of George's foot had squished the flesh out of the skin, greasing the pavement and forming a little slipway.

'At least there weren't two of them,' smiled George. 'Then I'd have a pair of slippers.'

'Boom, boom!' laughed Grandpa Jock, 'But that's as close to a banana as I'll get to these days. They clog up my insides.'

'What do you mean, Grandpa?' quizzed George.

'Well, let's just say that bananas have an anti-laxative effect, lad, the older you get.' Grandpa Jock raised one of his bushy ginger eyebrows and looked down on George.

'You mean you're not as regular as you used to be, Grandpa?' sniggered George.

'I'm as regular as ever I was, thank you very much,' he blustered, his ginger moustache fluttering up and down. 'Regular as clockwork, young man! It's just that, well, bananas are, er… a bit more difficult to digest for us oldies.'

'You mean they're not so easy to slip out, Grandpa?' said George mimicking his banana slip.

Grandpa Jock and George were still laughing and pretending to slide on imaginary banana skins as they turned the corner at the end of the street and bumped into a family coming out of Little Pumpington's only fast food burger restaurant, McDoballs. Their arms were stuffed with bags of cheeseburgers, hamburgers, French fries, double quarter pounders and big cups of juice; everybody had an extra-large sized container of a bright pink liquid. Grandpa Jock nudged George and whispered...

'And talking of bad diets, you couldn't pay me to eat that junk, even with me teeth in.' He went on, 'It's not even real meat, it's all the left-over waste bits, padded out with straw.'

'But did you see their drinks too, Grandpa. Fruit juice! As if that would make those burgers healthier? Greasy burgers and fruit juice? No chance!' George didn't really like burgers; he'd never really got the taste for them.

'And,' Grandpa Jock looked about them suspiciously, 'there's poo in the burgers!'

'There is not!'

'I promise you, lad. They put cow poo into the burgers, with straw and hay to pad them out a bit, to make all the meaty mush go further.' Grandpa Jock turned his head, just in case the burger police were listening. 'It's all part of the processing in their secret recipe. All the scrapings from the barn floor.'

'No way, that's disgusting.' George stuck his tongue out and pretended to gag, a little gurgle strangling in his throat.

'Aye way, laddie. I've read aboot it. Those mad McDoballs people want to take over the world and force everyone to eat hamburgers everyday till we're all so fat we burst!' Grandpa Jock squeezed the palms of his hands over his puffed up cheeks and pressed hard until his tongue burst from his mouth in a large explosion of raspberry parping noise and spittle. This was closely followed by a top set of false teeth - almost.

Grandpa Jock pulled his hand over his mouth and quickly shoved his dentures back into place before they could escape.

At that moment, another loud parping noise could be heard coming towards them from the other side of a large, blue wooden fence. The parade ground was just around the corner.

'Was that an elephant's trumpet, Grandpa?' asked George

'Not sure lad, but it's better than a trouser trumpet.'

Grandpa Jock always laughed at his own jokes, whether they were funny or not. George shared his grandfather's toilet sense of humour.

'I've read that the monkeys in this circus have been taught to play the trumpet, Grandpa,' said George, before realising his mistake. George had opened the door for one of his Grandpa's poems; never original, usually rude and always capable of making the old prankster laugh. He never missed an opportunity to slot one into conversation, usually to George's mum's great offence. And George had heard this one a thousand times.

'Not last night, but the night before,' he sang.

'Three little monkeys came to my door,' George was getting ready to join in.

'One with a trumpet, one with a drum,' Grandpa Jock steadied himself for the last line.

'And one with a pancake stuck up his bum!' Grandpa Jock and George shouted triumphantly as they walked around the corner into the parade ground.

Twenty people turned to look around in disgust at the tuneless, cheeky warblings of the pair of laughing idiots coming round the corner. George felt his face beginning to burn brightly with embarrassment, and what didn't help was that his slightly-larger-than-average ears began to glow red too. A small section of the large crowd in front of them just stared, as if they'd never seen anyone fooling around before.

Then Grandpa Jock let out a loud burp.

'Better out than in, I always say,' announced Grandpa Jock loudly. Affronted, most of the crowd turned their backs on Grandpa Jock as they tutted and huffed. Some of the little kids at the front were still looking at the wild-haired funny man and put their hands over their mouths to stifle laughter that their parents certainly wouldn't approve of.

Pretending to be shocked by this behaviour, George exclaimed, 'Well, really, Grandfather! What do you say?'

'I'd usually say "Cor, that was a loud one!"' replied Grandpa Jock, laughing again at his own hilarity. Most of the little kids thought it was funny too.

The parp of a trumpet interrupted Grandpa Jock's comic routine and the crowd gasped and began to strain their necks. George couldn't see too much as Grandpa Jock pulled him by the arm down to the bottom of the field, stepping over a couple of very mushy pineapples in the process.

Chapter 2 – The Parade

ton's parade ground isn't really a parade
ch. It's more of a car park, next to a football
pitch, alongside a large patch of wasteland. There weren't
too many parades around these days either but once a
year the travelling shows arrived with their Waltzers and
Dodge'ems and a Haunted House that wasn't all that scary.
And on the third Sunday of every month, the local farmers'
market would pitch up to sell their wares; fresh fruit and
vegetables and the like. You could tell they were fresh
because they were usually still covered in manure.

George wondered if the farmers were responsible for
leaving the rotten fruit lying around for people to slide on
but realised that the north east corner of England didn't
really have the climate to grow pineapples, never mind
bananas. Little Pumpington's farmers tended to grow
turnips and potatoes and other root vegetables.

Grandpa Jock fought his way through the thickest part
of the crowd away from the parping noises and over to the
edge of the football pitch, where the number of on-lookers
began to thin out, due to the mucky, underfoot conditions;
no one wanted to stand in the mud. George and Grandpa
Jock were able to step right up to the rope, that was
used to keep the crowds back from the parade, giving
them a clear view, even though the puddles came up
over their toes.

'That's why you wanted me to wear my wellies, Grandpa,'
realised George.

'Up there for thinking,' said Grandpa Jock pointing to his
forehead, 'Down there for dancing.' And he shoogled his
large black wellington boots back and forth in a shuffly kind
of dance, splashing puddle water everywhere.

'Here they come,' shouted George, pointing at the large

ringmaster striding round the bend with a long whip in his hand and his big, fat belly protruding in front of him. He wore a shiny pink top-hat and pink tuxedo jacket with two long tails flowing behind. He had on a white shirt, beneath a black cummerbund which was stretching to the point of bursting; he wore black britches tucked into pink leather boots.

Behind him came a procession of elephants, the first swinging its trunk from side to side in a slow plodding manner. The elephant was wearing a triangular piece of coloured material on its head with little red tassels around the edges. Embroidered in the centre of cloth was the word 'Nelly' – very original, George thought.

She was the large matriarch of a four-strong herd of circus elephants. The other three elephants followed Nelly's pace, with the smallest calf bringing up the rear. Nelly the Elephant's eyebrows were crossed and her eyes were downcast, as if she was embarrassed to be seen in public wearing the jumbo equivalent of a knotted hanky.

Behind Nelly was another enormous elephant, with huge ears and two long ivory tusks protruding out in front. 'Smelly' was printed her hanky and behind her was a smaller elephant, with delicate, even petite little ears. This elephant seemed to glide like a princess. Grandpa Jock whispered to George…

'Those front two are African elephants. The third one is an Indian elephant.'

'How can you tell, Grandpa?'

'Size, lad. Size of their bodies, size of their ears, size everything,' said Grandpa Jock.

George stared at his grandfather, quite impressed.

'Oh, that…' Grandpa Jock went on, 'plus the fact that they've called her 'Delhi'. Look, it's printed onto the big hanky on her forehead. And look at this one…'

George turned. 'Nelly, Smelly and Delhi,' he groaned.

At the back of the parade was the tiniest, cutest elephant in the history of adorable grey mammals. The little jumbo wobbled, instead of walked and stitched onto the red headdress was the word 'Jelly' – Jelly the Elephant, thought George. Jelly the Baby Elephant; Jelly Baby! There was a pink ribbon weaved through the elephant's tail and false eyelashes had been stuck on her face.

'Hang on, those are fake lashes,' shouted George. 'Someone's cashing in on the cute factor.'

'That's a bit cynical, George,' replied Grandpa Jock. 'It's only a bit of fun...'

But Grandpa Jock was interrupted by a deafening trumpet blast. George couldn't tell if this was from an elephant or from a real trumpet but it signalled the start of the madness. On top of Smelly's back was a bright yellow box and from it jumped a pair of the most mischievous primates George had ever seen.

The first chimp was wearing enormously baggy, red trousers with white spots and they were held up with striped braces. Around the waist of the baggy trousers looked like a hoola-hoop, pushing the waist-band out wider and making the monkey look more ridiculous than ever. The ankles of the trousers were pulled tight to exaggerate the chimp's saggy bottom. On the chimp's head was a green bowler hat with the name 'Pippo' written across the front.

Pippo had just climbed out of the box and hopped down to Nelly's bottom and yanked her tail furiously. This caused the unhappy jumbo to parp out another loud blast from its trunk.

'Look what that monkey did, George,' said Grandpa Jock pointing. The second chimp saw him waving his finger and copied him. Then it pulled its large ears out wide and stuck out his tongue.

'It's not a monkey, Grandpa. It's a chimpanzee,' corrected

George. 'Monkeys have tails.' Maybe Grandpa Jock's nature knowledge wasn't as extensive as he'd first pretended.

'Well, they're all the same to me,' moaned Grandpa Jock, 'Monkeys, apes or chimps; I bet they don't dress up like that in the jungle.'

But the chimp was still trying to catch Grandpa Jock's attention, and as soon as Grandpa Jock looked up the chimp jumped to its feet, turned round, pulled his baggy clown pants down and flashed his hairy bum.

Zippy was the younger of the two chimps. George knew he was called Zippy because his yellow bowler hat had the word 'Zippy' printed across the front. He was also wearing a huge pair of size 35 clown's shoes, which made him clumsy and awkward.

Pippo was clearly the chimp-in-charge, with wisps of white hair around his greying beard. He carried a golden bugle strapped over one shoulder but what lessened the air of authority was his annoying habit of picking his nose and pulling out large monkey bogies; big and green and occasionally strung out with bits of snot. At this point, Pippo would have a choice; flick the monkey booger towards the crowd or to eat it. The old chimp seemed to prefer the latter.

'That must be Pippo and Zippy. They own this circus, you know,' shouted Grandpa Jock.

'Don't be daft, Grandpa. How can two nose-picking chimpanzees own a circus?' asked George.

'If anyone knows about amazing animals, it's those two chimps,' Grandpa Jock replied with childlike bewilderment. George just stared at his grandpa in disbelief. Surely he didn't think that these two mischief makers were in charge of the whole circus? Did he?

The chimps were just one notch down on the evolutionary ladder but George reckoned it was quite a big notch.

In fact, he thought about the gaping chasm between managing a travelling commercial business and just throwing poo at the audience in the name of entertainment.

'Fantastically cunning little business monkeys,' winked Grandpa Jock.

George stared at the chimpanzees; they certainly seemed to know what they were doing, hopping down from their box with buckets and spades in their paws but they hardly looked like the joint heads of a major corporation.

Before he could ask, the crowd began to groan and snigger, and several people started holding their noses. This was not going to be pleasant.

With a resigned air of sadness and relief, Smelly the Elephant lifted up her tail and dropped an enormous splodge of poo out of her bottom. Large wet blobs began plunking downwards and squelching into a big pile on the floor.

Plop after plop emerged from Smelly's bottom, great whiffs of steam rising up from the shimmering mass. The ringmaster's face was purple with rage; clearly upset that Smelly had relieved herself in front of an audience. The only problem was....

George stared at the poo with his eyes wide open and his mouth gaping. 'Grandpa, look at the poop!' Grandpa Jock was equalled shocked and his top set of teeth dropped down, almost falling out of his mouth again.

The great steaming dollop of elephant's dung was bright pink!

With well-drilled precision, Pippo raised his bugle and blew as hard and as furiously as his fat monkey lips would allow. Zippy quickly but carefully, aware of the tripping hazard of size 35 shoes, began shovelling, shifting and scooping up the mess on the floor, popping the poop into the plastic buckets.

When one bucket was filled Pippo would hop up and store it securely in the box on the elephant's back, as Zippy filled the next one. There was a lot of poop to pick up but the chimps worked fast, making sure all of the sloppy sludge was collected. Not a drop was left on the floor and the dancing chimps finally swung back up into their box to a warm round of applause from the appreciative audience.

Grandpa Jock clapped enthusiastically. 'Well done, ya wee monkeys!' he shouted, clearly delighted that the chimps wanted to keep the streets of Little Pumpington poop-free.

'They've cleaned up after the elephants but why is the poo pink, Grandpa?' asked George.

'Well, I don't know,' muttered Grandpa Jock, still staring and clapping at the parade, 'Maybe they're all girl elephants?' Grandpa Jock never seemed terribly bright when it came to these matters.

The McDoballs Corporation

From: *Chief Operating Officer*
To: *All Department Executives*
Subject: Operation Addictive Elephant Project X

Ladies and gentlemen,

As you are all aware, we have invested heavily in our latest Project X and are now ready to increase production levels. Each department has a key role in successfully achieving maximum profitability; read now and make it happen!

Marketing: *Ensure public awareness reaches new record highs by the end of the month, creating consumer desire and demand for Product X. That means the public must know about it and want to buy it.*

Marketing: *Use new advertising campaign to manipulate the environmentally and eco-friendly consumer, and to compliment all our other products in the marketplace.*

Production: *Final instalment of the farm's production process will be complete tomorrow. Expect delivery tonight and be running at full capacity within 48 hours.*

Distribution: *Ensure this increase in production is delivered to our customer-facing outlets at once.*

Finance: *Our sales forecasts are not ambitious enough. Double sales targets immediately!*

Operations: *In your last memo, you stated that we were in the hands of Mother Nature. Well, Mother Nature needs to be reminded of our new sales targets. You're fired! Pack your desk and remove yourself from the building tout-suite. The new Director of Operations will be in place tomorrow morning, if not sooner.*

All: *Finally, it goes without saying that absolute secrecy must be maintained. Our consumers are easy prey, allowing us to sell an addictive product to greedy people. We must remain ruthlessly hidden behind our faceless corporate identity, in order to see our bank account bulge as big as our customers' bellies.*

Or else!

Yours sincerely
C.O.O.

I'M STUFFIN' IT

Chapter 4 – The Parade Continues

George was left scratching his head as the rest of the huge parade passed slowly by.

Now and again other elephants would feel the call of nature and to the crowd's great hilarity, take another pink dump on the ground. The bugle would sound enthusiastically and the two chimps would swing into action once more. Always efficient and effective, the monkey shovellers would scrape up every last piece of poo into their buckets; leaving a delicate pink stain on the pathway but not a piece of poop in sight.

At last the procession of elephants, the chimpanzees and all other circus acts romped passed by the cheering crowds, walking around the football pitches towards the Big Top Tent that was set up the end of the field. Grandpa Jock and George started to walk back towards the main road, slowly, as the rest of the crowd shuffled its way through the patch of wasteland.

George glanced over to his left and screwed his eyes up narrowly, peering over to the road. He wrinkled his nose and stared intently at the ground. Then, with a swift step, he lifted his leg over the rope and crossed over the barrier. Grandpa Jock was not slow to notice this but he had more difficulty in lifting his leg up. The rope was just too high. He tried to bend down but the same rope was just too low.

'Ooyah, George,' he groaned, and George turned, stepped back across to the rope and lifted it as high as he could. Grandpa Jock stooped slightly and crept forward.

"I couldn't get me old leg over,' groaned Grandpa Jock.

'Well, you should've used your younger leg then,' sniggered George. Grandpa Jock just snarled, almost breaking into a smile, as he fought to keep control of his curling lips and loosening teeth.

George was quickly back over to the centre of the path, kneeling down and stretching his hand out, almost touching the rose red stain on the ground where the elephant's dump had been.

'Urgh, watch out, lad! That's where the poo was,' shouted Grandpa Jock, wondering why his gormless grandson would want to play with poo. Grandpa Jock's fat nostrils twitched... something smelled lovely.

'Elephant poo is meant to be green, isn't it, Grandpa? Or brown?'

'Usually, lad.'

'And how does it normally smell?'

'Awful!' replied Grandpa Jock, 'I once went to a zoo in the middle of summer and it stunk to the heavens. But jumbo jobby is meant to be good for the garden though.'

'What's a jobby, Grandpa.'

'You should know that, lad,' tutted Grandpa Jock. 'It's my favourite Scottish word... it means 'poo'.'

'So why is this poo pink?' puzzled George, 'and why does it smell so, so....'

'Delicious?' suggested Grandpa Jock,

'Flowery - I was going to say, Grandpa.'

Grandpa Jock was lost in his own little world and stood licking his lips, 'Hmmm, it smells good enough to eat.'

George raised a disgustingly curious eyebrow towards his grandpa. Perhaps his grandpa should try expanding his diet in a healthier direction, he thought.

'And elephant dung is really useful stuff too, lad,' nodded Grandpa Jock. 'Dung can be recycled to make paper and all sorts of stuff.'

'Paper?' George's eyes widened.

'Yeah, look,' and Grandpa Jock pulled a little paperback book out from his coat pocket. Grandpa Jock loved reading and he always had a book on the go. He handed it to George.

'Go on,' he urged. 'Sniff the pages!'

'You mean the pages of this book are made from elephant dung!' George held the book up to his nose and sniffed. 'These pages here? These ones?'

'Elephants are generally vegetarians, right?' Grandpa Jock started to explain, 'so their dung is basically grass and leaves all mushed up. In Thailand and places like that, they collect elephant poo, squeeze all the water out of it, roll it out flat and pulp it into paper.'

'But this book here? The book in my hands, right now?' George was now holding the paperback out at arm's length, wondering where the pages actually came from. 'This one is made out of elephant poop?'

'Pretty cool, eh,' Grandpa Jock giggled. 'Sniff it and see...'

'Doesn't really smell of anything,' said George. He loved the fact that his grandpa was a walking encyclopaedia of useless knowledge, full of interesting yet utterly meaningless wisdom.

'And did you know,' he went on, 'that if you could pass wind continuously for seven years, you'd create as much energy as an atomic bomb!'

George looked shocked. 'Really, Grandpa.'

'Yeah,' replied Grandpa Jock, 'but don't try it. I once squeezed out a pump for just seven seconds and I nearly followed through in my pants.'

George rolled his eyes. 'But that doesn't change why the poo was pink. That's not normal?' he argued.

'Well, like I said, laddie, maybe they were girl elephants?' sighed Grandpa Jock.

'That doesn't work, Grandpa. Female elephants don't do pink poo any more than male elephants do blue poo. No animal does, for that matter.'

Grandpa Jock thought for a minute. 'Maybe they've been drinking too much red wine,' he suggested helpfully.

'I've heard of Indian elephants getting drunk on fermenting rice wine. Maybe that's what turned the poo pink?'

George wasn't sure and he eyed his grandpa suspiciously.

'Or maybe they put too much tomato ketchup on their hay,' groaned George.

'They might've done. Or maybe they've drunk too much cherryade?' Grandpa Jock was on a roll now, 'Or maybe they'd been eating crayons? I knew a dog once who curled out a very colourful creation after eating crayons.'

'Yeah, but red crayons, Grandpa? Really?' George was shaking his head.

'Maybe they're ill, internal bleeding or something.' suggested Grandpa, trying to be a little more sensible.

'I thought about that,' agreed George, 'but the elephants looked very healthy and blood turns poo black, not pink. This was a very bright pink.'

'Okay, okay,' nodded Grandpa Jock, 'let me think about it.'

Chapter 5 – Inside the Big Top

Inside the Big Top, Ronald the Ringmaster was furious. He stormed around the remaining performers, thrashing at the elephants with his long whip and threatening the two chimpanzees. Nelly the Elephant kept her head down and so did the rest of the herd. All the other animals had ducked for cover and ran off, leaving only the main attractions of the parade to bear the brunt of his fury.

'I told you all to go to the toilet before we set off, didn't I?' he screamed, 'I warned you it would be a long journey. I said you should do your business before we left the tent. What did I warn you?'

Pippo began to raise his paw as if to answer Ronald's rhetorical question but he was whacked on the back of the head by the trunk of the elephant standing behind him. He thrust his paw down quickly.

'But oh no!' the Ringmaster squealed, ignoring Pippo, 'How would I know when you're likely to drop one? I mean, I've only studied your bellies and bums for the last twelve months!' What would I know about the bowel movements of Elephas Loxodanta?'

Now Zippy scratched his head and put his paw gingerly in the air.

'It's Latin for African elephants, monkey brain!' roared Ronald, irritated at being interrupted but secretly pleased he could show off. Then he shouted 'And that includes you, Delhi!'

Delhi the elephant kept her graceful, almost regal head down low.

His rant went on, 'I've only had my head so far up your bottoms for over a year that I can set my watch by your bowel movements!'

'Instead, I have to rely upon these poor excuses for

monkey butlers to scrape up all your excretions, into buckets, by Jove....from the ground, no less.....attracting all sorts of contaminants, just to get your jumbo jobbies back here.'

'Do you know how valuable this stuff is? Are you aware how much it costs to feed a herd full of elephants on a diet of cranberries, blueberries, raspberries, gooseberries and dangleberries? It's very expensive. I mean, it doesn't grow on trees, you know.'

The wide eyed Ringmaster stopped for a second, realising that cranberries, blueberries, raspberries and gooseberries did grow on trees, or at least bushes (Dangleberries were another matter. Ask your dad about dangleberries) but he was really talking about the money, the time, the investment and the expertise involved in this project.

Ronald the Ringmaster continued to walk amongst the cowering animals, his hands clasped behind his back and kicking up sawdust as he strode around. He enjoyed being the centre of attention.

'But you're too stupid to appreciate that,' he snarled, smoothing his handlebar moustache down with one hand; the moustache occasionally bounced up and down, as if it had a life of its own.

'Thank goodness I have the creativity, the foresight and the genius to hire laboratory chimps clever enough to clear up the mess after you.'

The elephants hung their heads in shame, aware that their behaviour had somehow upset the man who was kind enough to give them a delicious daily diet their jungle cousins would have gladly given their trunks for. Or so the man in the pink jacket kept telling them.

'And this is how you pathetic pachyderms repay me...' the Ringmaster spat out the word pachyderms as if it were a nasty piece of phlegm caught at the back of his throat.

23

He was acutely aware that he'd only found out two months ago that 'pachyderm' was a posh word that meant 'elephant' in scientist speak but he didn't want his elephants knowing how ignorant he really was.

'...By dumping all over the road?!'

The elephants' ears burned red embarrassment. The chimps slapped at their trunks, chattering away, as if eagerly agreeing with the Ringmaster.

'Don't you realise? Nobody wants you. Nobody wants to see clumsy, oafish big brutes doing tricks for peanuts anymore. People don't even want to see elephants in zoos because it reminds them how cruel zoos are.'
The Ringmaster snapped his whip down against his boots once more.

'People think they are educated now. They pretend to have a conscience,' he said. 'People read on the internet how big an elephant's territory is in the wild. So, no matter how big your cage or enclosure is in a zoo, it still won't be big enough satisfy their guilt.'

'The rules have changed, my dumb friends. The government have foolishly passed laws banning animals in circuses and someone has to look after you. You have become a burden.'

Ronald lowered his voice to a whisper; the elephants recognised this cruel tone and avoided eye-contact. Even little Jelly knew to keep quiet.

'No one wanted to look after a hulking herd of beasts with monstrous appetites and no commercial value; even your ivory is illegal to sell and too dangerous for the black market. You might be cute at that age,' he went on pointing at the baby elephant, adding, 'But you'll grow. Then you'll be worthless.' The Ringmaster began to raise his voice again, this time triumphantly. The monkeys began chattering with bum-kissing enthusiasm.

'You were worse than worthless because it is very expensive to kill and dispose of a six ton mammal. Do you realise the size of a grave that's needed just to bury one of you? And nobody wants to see burning pyres of elephants smoking around the countryside.'

Even the Ringmaster thought he might have gone a little far there but he was hoping that his guilt-trip would force the elephants into behaving a little more gratefully than they had been.

'But I have arranged it all for you. I alone, have rescued you from the poachers axe, the burning scrapheap and the elephants' graveyard. I will take care of you; I will feed you luxuries beyond your wildest dreams in an elephant's paradise and all I ask is a little bit of co-operation from your bowel movements.'

'You will not even be alone! After this week, you will join the rest of my rescued herd in a huge sanctuary not far from here. I have gathered together every other elephant in the whole country at great expense and we will be one big happy, profitable family.' Ronald's eyes seemed to glow at the thought of pound notes and he went on, 'I will protect you and I will look after you.'

The chimps were now doing back flips with excitement.

'Soon, you will be safely under my control!' The glint in his eye was mesmerising. 'You will be wholly within my power, where your poop will be my poop! When you will do doo-doo, when I say you'll do a doo-doo! And you will feed on the juiciest feasts known to any elephant and I will wipe your gigantic bottoms as gratitude for my hard work!'

'Remember, I am your master!' he began shouting towards a crescendo, 'And your dung belongs to me!'

Chapter 6 – Pondering Pink Poo

George Hansen had lived in Little Pumpington all his life, in a small house with his mum and dad and until recently, with his older sister Henrietta who was now in her second year at University.

Since his sister had moved out, the house was less pink, less fluffy and less perfumy, which, to George's mind was good thing because his lungs could do with a break after the years of inhaling all the deodorant, body spray and hair products that his sister would leave lingering around in the bathroom every morning.

In fact, George could do with a break himself, after the excitement of the geriatric generator episode, the recent zombie epidemic in Little Pumpington and disappearance of all the town's old people and even Mr Jolly the Janitor. Then his school had exploded – twice!

The police had been expecting to find bits of Mr Jolly scattered around the countryside but nothing was ever found. Not even the smallest piece of him was discovered, apart from his smouldering, pink welly boots, which were ever so slightly singed around the top.

Grandpa Jock lived round the corner from George and there was more than a family resemblance between them. On a good day George could be best described as almost averagely good looking, some of the other kids in school would tease him, calling him 'Gorgeous George' but his Grandpa Jock, another less-than-perfect specimen, would say his face had character.

George guessed that in this case character meant ears sticking out every so slightly, one eye fractionally lower than the other and his mouth turning down, just a bit, at the side. He always thought he looked a bit like a badly put together Mr Potato-Head.

And ever since the first exploding school episode the old Scotsman had developed wild ideas about crazy conspiracies everywhere. George was worried his grandpa was beginning to lose his marbles.

He'd always been a little mad, the old Scotsman. He liked to burp the alphabet and his favourite game was trying to pee successfully in the dark, using only his sense of hearing as a guide. Grandpa Jock was comfortable to be around and George loved him for it; in the same way a dog loves its smelly old blanket; safe, warm and familiar.

But recently Grandpa Jock had become paranoid, talking about undercover governments and secret corporations trying to take over the world. Grandpa Jock even tried to persuade George that we'd never sent a man to the moon; that it was all a big trick.

Grandpa Jock insisted the American government had captured UFO's and kept them hidden in an underground bunker in the desert. He said he'd been to Area 51 and madder yet was his claim that aliens living amongst us.

Worst of all, Grandpa Jock had almost been arrested for pulling the wig off the head of a very tall thin man with huge hands, claiming he wanted to prove the existence of aliens living in Little Pumpington. But the man wasn't an alien, just a very tall, bald man with big hands and rather self-conscience about his lack of hair.

The police were sympathetic on that occasion but George's mum and dad had threatened to throw him in an old folks' home, or worse, if he went doolally. Now Grandpa Jock only mentioned the conspiracies theories that surrounded him to George.

'Why is a conspiracy called conspiracy?' Grandpa Jock would insist. 'I'll tell you, George. "Con" means "'against" George, that's what it means. "Against."'

'And then there's the 'piracy' bit' Grandpa Jock would

quibble. 'You see, cons – piracy. Pirates! It's the pirates of big business that are against us. Just like real pirates, a bunch of crooks, willing to steal your hard-earned cash straight out of your pocket. Big businesses, like the banks, have been doing it for years. They're thieving bandits, George!' He'd get quite animated, arguing with himself.

'Big businesses, that's who's against us, the little people. Big businesses, like that online Amazing book company or Stirblacks Coffee or Micro-pad or whoever; they're all pirates! Stealing, thieving big companies, who wriggle out of paying tax, cheat their customers… and their staff… and the little man in the street.'

'There's pirates all round about us, George! Watch out for them.' Then he'd wink…'You can't spell conspiracy without lots of "cons" and a bit o'piracy. Think about it. Yarrrrrrrr!'

Grandpa Jock would curl his lip up and roll the growl of the 'Yarrrrrrrr!' around the back of his throat like a salty old sea-dog and George would begin to believe his grandpa really had gone a bit mad.

Chapter 7 – To Date, Or Not To Date

The journey back from the parade-ground had taken twenty minutes and Grandpa Jock spent most of the time explaining to George why he believed fast food chains put poo in their burgers. He'd been delighted to be proved right over the whole horse burger scandal a few years ago but George didn't really fancy finding out the truth about poo.

'Urgh, don't, Grandpa,' groaned George. 'I'm supposed to be going to McDoballs tonight with Kenny. You'll put me right off my food.'

'I don't think that's possible, lad,' laughed Grandpa Jock, and George fired him a narrow-eyed stare.

Unfortunately, George wasn't looking where he was going and as they turned the corner he bumped straight into a tall, dark haired girl.

'Allison!' yelled George.

'George!' squealed Allison. 'You're standing on my toes, George!'

George jumped back, apologising profusely but it was Allison who was looking rather red-faced.

George and Allison had been good friends since she'd moved to Little Pumpington last year. She was the only girl who'd ever been able to make George cry but he always denied it, saying he had some porridge in his eye. George had been put off females at a very young age, after a malicious bunch of older girls had given him the nickname 'Gorgeous George', which meant he usually kept the entire other half of the species at arms length. But Allison was pretty cool.

Now George looked her squarely in the face and watched her cheeks redden

'You'll catch flies in that mouth, George Hanson' said Allison, with her head held high.

George snapped his teeth together painfully, suddenly aware that his mouth was hanging open like a slack-jawed yokel.

'What's the matter? Never seen a girl going out on a date before?' Allison strode towards him haughtily.

'Urrggh, you? A date?' groaned George, becoming ever so slightly self-conscience as he said it. 'But you're only eleven!'

'So what?' snapped back Allison, 'My mum says I'm growing into a young lady and if a boy wants to take me out on a date, then why not?'

'But I mean, who'd want to take you out on a date?' George didn't mean to sound defensive. Surely he wasn't jealous, was he? No, not a bit, definitely not, absolutely no chance; he tried to convince himself but Allison hadn't noticed. She was looking up the street at a boy walking towards them. He was wearing a smart leather jacket that was slightly too big for him. His jeans were fresh and sharp and his hair had been combed flat over his head.

George reckoned that the lad's mother had probably dressed and prepared the boy, ready for his first date and had over-compensated in every department. In a futile attempt to regain some street cred, the boy had tried to mess up his hair at the front, spiking it in strange directions.

'Hang on a minute,' chuckled George. 'That's Crayon Kenny!'

Allison's face went redder. 'Stop calling him that. I know he's your friend but...'

'Yeah, but I mean... Crayon Kenny?' George was relieved that the competition for the girl he pretended he didn't fancy was one of the most unpredictably idiotic boys he'd ever met.

On a good day Kenny Roberts could be described as slightly eccentric. On other days Kenny could be certified as stark raving bonkers. Kenny was famous, both in school and all around Little Pumpington for his unusual hobby of sticking crayons, Brussel sprouts, peas, cornflakes and pretty much anything else up his nose and sometimes into other orifices around his body. Most of the nurses and doctors at Little Pumpington General Hospital were on first name terms with his parents and it was rumoured that they had a special pair of forceps with Kenny's name on them.

'Did they ever manage to find all the marbles that were stuck up his bottom?' giggled George. Allison didn't think this was funny but clearly she'd heard about 'the bag of marbles incident'. The look on her face suggested that she wished she hadn't told George she was going out on a date with the boy who was, allegedly, still discussing his 'achievement' with the Guinness Book of Records.

'Hi Allison, hi George,' smiled Kenny as he stepped up onto the pavement.

'Hey Kenny, what's up?' smirked George. Allison shot him a vicious look.

'Nothing yet,' replied Kenny with a wink, 'but the night is still young. I hear McDoballs have really bendy straws.'

George and Kenny started to laugh together. If Allison was a dragon, she'd be breathing fire by now.

Then George stood up straight. 'You're going on a date to a burger restaurant? Classy, Kenny.'

'We're not going on a date!' shouted Kenny with a shrill in his voice. 'Who said we were going on a date? It's not a date, my mum and dad need to take my little brother to hospital and they asked Allison's mum to watch me for a few hours. That's all.'

'So it's not a date?' George looked both puzzled and slightly amused.

'It's almost a date,' said Allison, now it was her turn to get defensive.

'It's nothing like a date,' replied Kenny, starting to look nervous in case there might be some hand-holding involved. 'You're coming too, mate. You said we'd go for a burger.' Kenny was hoping for male morale support.

'But I didn't know Allison was going to be there,' stammered George.

'No, George. You'd be a gooseberry,' insisted Allison. 'Two's company, three's a crowd.'

'But I like crowds,' choked Kenny, panic rising in his throat

Just then, Allison's mum popped her head out of the front door. She had curlers in her hair, her head was wrapped in a towel and she was wearing her dressing gown.

'Allison, did you lift the money I left for you on the kitchen table?' she shouted over.

'Your mum's paying for your date?' smiled George.

'It's not a date,' persisted Kenny.

'Yes, Mum,' called Allison. 'And it is too, Kenny Roberts.'

'Oh, there's George,' shrieked Allison's mum. 'Hi George!' and she began waving frantically. Allison rolled her eyes to the back of her head; honestly, parents can be so embarrassing sometimes. Worse was yet to come. Allison's mum had stepped outside and was now bustling along towards the gate. Allison groaned and put her face in her hand.

'There you are, George. Why don't you go for a burger with these two?' Allison's mum began pushing the three of them along the pavement towards town.

'Go on now, Allison has plenty of money with her,' she insisted. George reckoned she wasn't taking no for an answer.

She bent down and whispered in Allison's ear, 'Look, I'm only looking after Kenny as a favour to his mum. I don't want that nose-picking little nutcase in my house for any longer than is necessary. Understand?'

Then she straightened her back and readjusted the towel around her head. She looked a little flustered, hoping no one (especially Kenny) had overheard her guilty secret. Allison's mum was very house-proud and certainly didn't want to find crispy bogies rubbed into her white leather sofa, or anywhere else for that matter.

'You kids just have fun tonight. Stay out as long as you like.' Allison's mum was still prodding Allison down the street and Allison was ushering the boys in front.

George was swept along with Kenny, realising it was easier to go with the flow; Allison had accepted her fate, that her date wasn't a real date and Kenny was relieved that it had been finally settled.

'Oh, and Allison, remember what Kenny's dad said on the phone? About crayons and straws and things.....' Allison's mum now looked a little unsure. 'Just keep an eye on him, okay?' And she bustled back into the house.

'Come on then,' grumped Allison walking away dejectedly, her daydream shattered.

'What's wrong with your little brother then?' asked George, turning to Kenny.

'Well, you know those little toy soldiers you get? The green ones?' said Kenny intriguingly. 'Do you know how many a four year old can stick up their bottom? At least five!'

'Five!' laughed George, impressed that Kenny had the persuasive powers to talk his little brother into such a stunt.

'You must be very proud,' snapped Allison haughtily and she started to walk on ahead. George smiled and nodded with a wink of appreciation.

'I told him they were in the Pooperchute Regiment,' chuckled Kenny.

Allison groaned and walked faster.

Chapter 8 – Zombie Zone

When they came around the corner at McDoballs, the burger bar was absolutely bursting at the seams. The queue was right out of the door and the three of them joined at the back. Every seat in the restaurant was taken and people were feeding their faces frantically. Others were running outside with bags of takeaways in their arms, desperate to start munching in their cars and the drive-thru was queued right around the building. McDoballs was a very popular place.

Through the window George could see customers shovelling handfuls of chips into their mouths. Most of the chips were smothered in a kind of cheese; the warm runny mush that George's dad dipped his nachos into at the cinema.

The diners, no matter how hard they practised, couldn't open their mouths wide enough to avoid covering their chins with the yellow sauce. Cheese and ketchup was all over their hands, down the front of their t-shirts and splattered over all the tables.

Part of the problem was that most of the diners were too greedy; not knowing when they'd had enough but really because McDoballs had installed a self-pump cheese dispenser in the centre of the restaurant besides the napkins the straws, knifes and forks. People couldn't help themselves... well, they could, that was the whole point of a self service pumper but they couldn't stop themselves from pumping out more and more cheese.

Sure, McDoballs had provided little paper cups for customers to use but they weren't big enough. Customers had taken to filling up empty juice cups with cheese and were dunking their burgers in, scooping up great dollops of thick yellow gloop.

As the queue inched closer to the till, finally moving

through the double doors, George could see that every customer was munching some type of burger from the McDoballs menu. Despite the fact that there were posters of salads, carrot sticks and apple slices around the walls, nobody was eating that 'healthy muck', as one customer put it. Everyone was tucking into cheeseburgers, double cheeseburgers, double hamburgers with extra cheese, triple burgers with bacon and/or extra cheese.

It was like a feeding frenzy at the zoo, as if a zookeeper had thrown a bucket of sardines into the sea lions' enclosure, as long as the fish had been dipped in cheese first.

And everyone was washing down their chips and burgers with extra large cups of fruit juice!

George thought for a moment, and then asked 'Why isn't anyone drinking fizzy cola?'

'Come on, George,' groaned Kenny, 'where have you been? Haven't you heard of this new health juice? It's called the Power Pink Drink. You can only buy it in McDoballs AND it helps you lose weight.'

'No way!' gasped George looking around, 'I don't think it's working then.' George stared at all the diners and sure enough, most of them were a bit on the large side. Some of them were on the huge side and a few of them were on the gargantuan, borderline breaking-the-bench side.

Allison pointed to a large colourful poster on the wall that advertised 'Power Pink' in bold bright lettering.

The slogan read…

'Power Pink, Power Pink - the more weight you'll lose, the more Power Pink you drink!'

Underneath the neon, almost eye-dazzling headline was a paragraph of additional sales information.

'From Nature's Larder! Power Pink is the all natural, fruit based health drink, specially blended from a secret combination of wholesome and nourishing ingredients. Actively works with your body to burn off those unwanted calories. (*when used as part of a calorie controlled diet) It's fresh and filtered by Mother Nature, for a pure, captivating flavour.'

'Apparently, it's true,' said Allison, relieved that the boys had finally started talking about a 'normal' subject. 'McDoballs launched it a couple of weeks ago and it's supposed to slow down your metabolic rate.'

'Metabobble bubble what? grimaced George.

'Your metabolic rate,' went on Allison, deliberately slowing down her sentence as if she was talking to a three year old. 'That means the speed at which your body burns off fat.'

'Some of these people could use a bonfire then,' replied George.

'And the taste of the juice is supposed to compliment every burger in McDoballs. That's why this place is so popular,' added Kenny. 'It's almost addictive.'

George raised an eyebrow. He was pretty certain that he wasn't going to become addicted to a load of greasy hamburgers, no matter how tasty the pink drink thingy was. They were almost at the front of the queue.

'What are you two having then?' asked Allison.

'I'll go for the bagel burger meal,' drooled Kenny, 'large size with a Power Pink, please.'

'I'm still thinking,' said George staring up at the menu board, unsure if he would actually like anything on the list.

'Well, hurry up George. It's our turn.' They had reached the front of the queue. Allison turned to server behind the counter.... 'One big Bagel Burger meal, with a Power Pink please. I'll have a regular Mad Mac meal with a diet Power Pink and he'll have.... What do you want to eat, George?' Allison was getting impatient now. To Allison, fast food should be ordered quickly too. George was still staring up at the board.

'I'll just have the, errrr, the...' George mumbled, still unsure what to order. Nothing looked or sounded appetizing to him. He stared up at the board and began to feel people behind him getting impatient. He had to decide now and there were even pictures of each burger to help him choose.

Should he go for the Squeeze Burger – a burger so large you had to use both hands to squash it down until it would fit in your mouth? Should he try the Peas Burger; from the healthy option range; a burger served with mushy peas instead of onions? Would he like the Grease Burger, as it seemed to be one of the most popular, judging by the number of people stuffing them into their mouths around the restaurant

'I'll just go for a plain hamburger please,' said George finally. 'Oh, and a portion of chips.'

'Fries,' said the spotty teenager in the paper hat.

George looked down at the zipper on his trousers, then back to the server. 'Excuse me?' he asked.

'Not chips, fries!' the server insisted. 'You have to ask for 'fries"

'Why?' asked George.

'Because it sounds more American,' said the server. One of his spots looked like it was ready to erupt. 'It's cooler than saying 'chips'.'

'Ok, I'll have a portion of fries then,' said George sarcastically.

'Large or regular?'

'Just normal.' George was becoming bored with the whole ritual.

'What drink would like with that?' Spotty Server was now in the zone, asking questions automatically, without hesitation.

'Erm,' paused George, 'I'll just have some of hers.' He pointed to Allison, who was also relieved to have to whole ordering procedure over with and she stepped in front of him. George might be smart but sometimes he could be pretty dumb, she thought.

Allison handed money over to Spotty Server and George watched the other servers behind the long bank of checkouts. They were all of about the same age, all equally spotty but with various degrees of eruptability; some spots had huge yellow heads, ripe and ready to rupture, others were just red, swollen and freshly squeezed.

George wondered where McDoballs got their cheese from.

All the servers were at different stages of their transactions. George noticed that they all saying the same things, just at different times as if they'd been pre-programmed to utter a chosen phrase at each specific point.

'Kind of brainwashed, aren't they?' George looked at Kenny and nodded his head towards the servers.

'Not that they started with much brains, judging by this lot,' agreed Crayon Kenny.

'Nonsense, you two,' said Allison abruptly; carrying the tray passed the two boys. 'It's a perfectly good job for any student, working themselves through college or university. It's not too taxing and you get to eat as many burgers are you want. Well, the leftover ones, anyway"

'But they're so brain dead,' argued George.

'Like zombies,' agreed Kenny.

'Yeah, we're in the zombie zone,' laughed George. 'Even the customers look like the undead.'

'I wonder if they make brain burgers here,' said Kenny.

'Urgh, that's disgusting!' Allison groaned and rolled her eyes again. George thought she was dangerously close to becoming a teenager. 'You two can be so vile sometimes,' she added, putting the tray down on a recently vacated table. It was still covered in burger wrappers, empty paper cups and the obligatory cheese and ketchup spillages.

Allison sat down, clearing away the debris onto a tray; Kenny went off to the cheese stand and came back ten seconds later with three little cups of tomato sauce and a handful of napkins. The boys then plonked themselves down opposite. Allison and Kenny picked up their food, unwrapped their burgers and began to tuck in.

McDOBALLS

From: *Head of Marketing*
To: *Chief Operating Officer*
Cc: *Head of Operations*
Subject: Deflecting Public Opinion

Sir,

As part of our campaign to win the hearts and minds of the general public, whilst deflecting attention away from the company's 'other' operations, I suggest a marketing strategy whereby we organise a televised public relations broadcast at the production centre to show off our new sanctuary.

We will be able to manipulate the editorial content for this news item, to ensure the sanctuary is viewed in the most positive of lights, as a haven of tranquillity and pleasure for our latest arrivals. Under no circumstances will the true nature of the production centre be highlighted in this broadcast.

Although this is a necessary and advantageous public relations exercise, it will not detract from the ongoing operations at the production centre. Our Head of Distribution says current stocks are running low, due to the popularity of Product X and immediate replenishment of supplies is required urgently.

Yours sincerely
Head of Marketing

Chapter 10 – Taste Test

George poked his package, watching Allison and Kenny begin to munch into their food eagerly. As Kenny took a big bite of his burger, the large bottom of the person sitting next to him bumped him forward. A huge dollop of tomato ketchup squidged out of his bun, narrowly missed the table and splattered onto his jeans.

'It's OK, that's got to happen with the first bite,' he said nonchalantly, 'those are the rules.'

'What's that you're eating anyway,' asked George taking a closer look at Kenny's burger. It was round with a hole on the top, in the middle of the bun. Kenny lifted his burger to his mouth to take another bite and George saw another hole at the bottom.

'Itha maymal mummah,' mumbled Kenny with his mouth stuffed with burger.

'A what?'

'Ah maymal mummah!' He tried to say again, only succeeding this time in spraying bits of bun over the table.

'He said it's a bagel burger,' said Allison clearly, washing her burger down with a gulp of juice. 'It's one of McDoballs signature buns,' she went on. 'Designed to look like a doughnut, with a ring of beef patty, served with onions, ketchup and mustard on a glazed bagel bun. They've sold over a billion of them worldwide.'

'Oh, right,' said George, in burger ignorance. 'And what's that you've got?'

Allison held up her burger. 'It's a Mad Mac, another of their unique signature creations. Two regular burgers, served in a triple layer bun with peanut butter and jelly filling and a scattering of lettuce on each layer. It's delicious!'

George stared at her with a choking gag of sick forming in the back of his throat. 'You've got to be kidding me.'

'No. Here, try some,' and Allison pushed her bun across the table and slurped another mouthful of the purple drink in front of her.

'No, thanks all the same. I'll stick with this one,' said George, picking up his bun quickly and pulling the wrapping paper off it. His plain burger now seemed the safest option on the menu. He picked it up and sniffed it. It smelled beefy. George bit into it. It tasted... meaty but maybe not in a good way.

'It tastes like meat is supposed to taste, if you were trying to explain it to an alien who'd never tasted meat before,' George blurted out, with the ball of beef and bun pushed inside his cheek. He went on chewing carefully.

'Actually, now, after a few chews,' George chomped again, 'it's starting to taste more like... sawdust... from a butcher's floor.'

'Honestly, between the two of you,' Allison complained, 'this is not a pleasant dining experience.'

'Actually,' replied Kenny, 'I've never found eating in here a pleasant experience. I'm usually squished between two fat people, the seats are hard, the tables are messy and there are always chips, sorry, fries lying all over the place. I only come here for the burgers.'

'So why do you keep eating then,' puzzled George.

'I don't know,' replied Kenny,' it's probably just habit now. I've been coming since I was a baby.'

'They've certainly got you hooked,' said Allison, looking down her nose at him.

'My Grandpa Jock thinks burger companies pack their burgers full of sawdust and straw and er....other stuff... you know, cheaper ingredients, to make more profit.'

'Yeah, but sawdust?' complained Kenny.

'But what if the meat had no real taste anyway,' added George. 'Sawdust and straw would pad the burgers out and then they could add loads of artificial flavours afterwards.'

Allison started nodding her head and beginning to think George had a point. Kenny just kept stuffing his face with more burger.

'Better not say that too loud,' muffled Kenny, spitting more random bits of burger around. 'This mob will chuck us out if we start slagging off their burgers.'

Allison was now staring at her half-eaten burger in her hand. George could almost see the mental cogs of thought processing an idea in Allison's head. He watched Allison take a bite and she started munching on her latest mouthful of burger.

She kept on munching.

And munching.

And munching.

'And my Grandpa Jock says that there's poo in the burgers as well.'

Allison screwed up her face, looked around in disgust, wondering what to do with her mouthful of mush and with a gag, she spat the chewed up lump across the table. Kenny dodged to his left and it missed George's head by a fraction, splatting against the window behind him and stuck there.

'That's disgusting,' choked Allison.

'That's very unladylike,' smiled Kenny, impressed that she could spit that far.

'Sorry, it's just my Grandpa Jock's mad idea,' said George.

'No, I mean that burger was disgusting,' explained Allison. 'I'd been chewing that one bite for a while, until all the meaty flavour disappeared. Then, it did just taste like hay. Or sawdust, like you said.'

Allison reached for her juice and slurped a mouthful of the pink liquid up the straw to take the taste away. Kenny looked at the straw with interest.

'Wow! That was amazing,' gasped Allison. The two boys looked at each other.

'What was?' they both asked together.

'After chewing that burger for ages, it really started to taste horrid, as if I'd chewed all the flavour out of it,' explained Allison, 'but once I took a drink of the juice, the taste in my mouth was luscious, perfect even.'

'That's a bit weird,' said George.

'It's as if the burger and the drink were made to go with each other!' Kenny joined in. 'Like a marriage made in heaven.'

'Or in a laboratory somewhere,' muttered George, turning his nose up at the thought of his burger now.

'Yes, but they totally compliment each other,' gushed Allison, delighted with her discovery. 'Let's test this some more.' And she munched into another bite of her burger.

Kenny and George did the same. For a few moments the thought of poop in the burgers was forgotten.

George, Kenny and Allison had been chomping burger and slurping on Power Pink juice for 10 minutes. The remnants of their meals had been spat back into the wrappers as soon as all the flavours had been mushed out and all the juice had been drunk.

'I didn't eat all my burger, right,' said Kenny. 'I spat most of it out because after I chewed the life out of it. What was left tasted really gross.'

'But after a slurp of Power Pink,' Allison continued, 'the burger taste was superb and you felt hungry again.'

George went on, 'This stuff is so amazing, it's scary.'

'Terrifying, really.' agreed Allison. 'It's no wonder this place is so busy these days.'

'Tell me about the poop in the burgers, George,' asked Kenny, intrigued now at the change in his food.

'Yes, your grandpa's theory?' Allison joined in. George was encouraged.

'Well, he says it's more than a theory,' started George. 'He says he read about a book called Fast Food Nation by Eric Slurper or Schlosser or Shomeshing. This guy claims that the cows they kill to make burgers are cut up so fast it was only normal for some of the poop from the cows' intestines to end up in the burgers.'

'Urgh?!' screamed Allison and Kenny together.

'Yes, and this guy kept writing about it and nobody sued him so he's pretty sure it must be true.' George continued. 'They even made a movie about it.'

Allison's face was screwed up now, 'But no one wants to eat poop.'

'A-ha,' said George lifting his finger, 'that's because the meat from those cows is mashed into a pulp until all the real flavour is gone, then they throw flavour additives and chemicals back into the mix so all the burgers taste like burgers, the same all over the world.'

'Really?' asked Allison. 'That would explain our taste test then.'

Kenny was absent-mindedly scratching the inside of one of his nostrils with a plastic coffee stirrer, 'But how did that pink juice stuff make the burger taste better again?'

'Who knows?' muttered George, 'But I think the McDoballs scientists have been busy mixing up some secret recipes.'

'Either way,' decided Allison, 'I don't think I'll be eating another burger in here in the near future.'

Chapter 11 – Elephants on the move

The three of them cleared the cups, straws, napkins and regurgitated burgers from their table (Allison had removed the extra straws Kenny had hidden in his jacket pocket) and they fought their way to the exit. The restaurant seemed busier now than when they went in.

'Look at this place,' glowered Kenny. 'See how many people are eating in here.'

'Yeah, looks like they're all addicted too,' added Allison, a little sheepishly when she considered how keen she was to eat the Mad Mac earlier.

George pulled his jacket over his shoulders and urged the others, 'Come on; let's get away from this madhouse.' They walked to the end of the road and round towards the parade-ground.

When they arrived, they found Grandpa Jock jumping in puddles. Kenny laughed but George and Allison were used to the old Scotsman's erratic behaviour.

'Ah, there you are, lad. I've been waiting ages for you. And you've brought your wee friends.'

'Hi Grandpa,' beamed George.

'Hi Mr Jock,' smiled Allison.

'And if it's not the infamous Kenny Roberts?' gasped Grandpa Jock, 'Crayon Kenny, known throughout the world for his disappearing piece of Lego trick? Hello again.'

Kenny beamed proudly and nodded.

'You lot haven't been eating burgers again, have you?' asked Grandpa Jock.

Allison looked a little squeamish but Kenny wanted to know more. Grandpa Jock was happy to tell them everything he knew about McDoballs and all the other fast food manufacturers, about the horse meat scandal and the poo and all the other things that the burger companies had been getting away with for decades. In the end, Grandpa Jock added...

'And they have even created a special additive, a chemical called Mono-sore-bum Gloopy-muck or something like that, that makes everything tastes brilliant, no matter what it is.'

They all stared at Grandpa Jock, mouths gaping wide. They were all now certain that they'd put the taste additive to the test earlier that evening. They'd proved to themselves how fake the burgers were.

'We could be eating anything, Mr Jock, and we'd never know it,' gulped Allison.

'Aye but you'll not be eating them burgers again in a hurry, will ye?' winked Grandpa Jock.

'Mr Jock? Do you want to see these peanuts disappear?' asked Kenny, changing the subject and keen to show off his talents to an appreciative audience.

'Give me those!' and Allison grabbed a bag of monkey nuts out of Kenny's hand. 'Where did you get these from?'

'My mum gave them to me, in case we were going to feed the elephants,' Kenny tried to explain but an exasperated Allison was having none of it.

'Elephants!' shouted George, and they all turned towards the Big Top.

Grandpa Jock shook his head. 'You're too late,' he whispered. 'They've all gone.'

'Half an hour ago,' he went on. 'I watched some ringmaster guy and the two chimps pack the four elephants into the back of a large truck. It was quite a crush, I can tell you.'

'Poor elephants,' said Allison sadly.

'But where did they take them?'

'I expect they're off to their new home,' nodded Grandpa Jock. 'The new elephant sanctuary is only a couple of miles up that way. Those chimps own that too.'

'WHAT?!' shrieked George, Kenny and Allison together.

'It's true,' announced Grandpa Jock with his whiskers standing to attention. 'I researched this. Pippo and Zippy don't just own the circus. They are the joint heads of a major multi-national corporation!'

'Chimps don't run businesses,' argued Allison.

But the penny dropped for George. 'That's why you said they were "fantastic little business monkeys", at the parade. I thought it was rather cryptic, Grandpa.'

'Cryptic?' yelled Allison. 'It's cuckoo!'

'Yeah,' agreed Kenny, sadly wrinkling up his nose. 'As much as I love the idea of monkeys being in charge of things, it's not very likely, is it?'

'But it is true!' insisted Grandpa Jock, 'I checked it out on the Interweb thingy.'

'Oh yeah, Mr Jock,' groaned Allison sarcastically. 'Everything's true on the Internet.'

Kenny looked dubious, unsure if he believed that anyone aged between seventy four and ninety two could use the Internet properly. Although no one really knew how old Grandpa Jock was but George and Allison had seen his formidable grasp of new technology before.

'I don't know how or why but those chimps are the chief executives and managing directors of several large companies,' Grandpa Jock went on. 'Property companies, distribution services, food manufacturing, you name it!'

'But who'd want two chimpanzees in charge of their company,' groaned Allison. 'They can't speak and I doubt if they've got much business acumen.'

'What kind of men?' Kenny looked puzzled.

'Acumen! Business acumen,' Allison was becoming irritated again. 'It means knowledge and experience and smart thinking. Something you definitely do not possess and I doubt if those chimps have it either.'

'Be that as it may, lassie, I'm certain that those monkeys are on the board of directors for several big companies. Their names are listed on official documents on the companies register.' Grandpa Jock was obviously convinced but just as the mad old Scotsman was just about to explain his latest theory he was interrupted by a truck engine chugging around the other side of the tent.

'They're back,' whispered Grandpa Jock. 'Quick. Hide round here.'

They darted to the edge of the waste-ground, and Grandpa Jock shouted, 'Watch your feet!' and George managed to jump over another pile of pink elephant poo.

'The chimps must've missed that one,' murmured Grandpa Jock, as they ducked into the bushes.

Almost instantly the truck appeared round the corner. It pulled up, the engine stopped and Pippo and Zippy stepped out of the back. Two seconds later they were joined by Ronald the Ringmaster, who pulled the riding crop out of his pink wellington boot and whacked the chimp across the bum with it.

'And don't pee on the cages again,' he shouted. 'I have to touch those when we get back to the sanctuary!'

Was it the Ringmaster? The pink boots gave him away but there was something different. He was still wearing his britches but minus his jacket and shirt. His braces went over his shoulders but his trousers looked baggier than normal. That was it… his big tummy had disappeared!

Not that George had seen his bare stomach before but it was only normal to assume there was a bulbous belly under there. Allison and Kenny spotted it too.

Kenny yelped, 'Where's his tummy gone?'

'He's skinny!' squealed Allison.

'Maybe he's lost it in a crash diet?' suggested George without thinking.

'What? In less than a week? I told you something wasn't right here!' Grandpa Jock puffed out his chest, convinced that this time his suspicions were correct.

It was too dark to see his face properly and they were still quite a distance away but that didn't stop George, Kenny and Allison peering hard into the gloom, as the odd trio disappeared into the big tent.

'He looked familiar,' wondered Allison aloud, 'without his tummy, that is. I just can't place him.'

Chapter 12 – Burger Brainwashing

The following morning was the first day of the half term holidays.

After the four of them had walked back from the parade-ground last night, almost in silence, George, Allison and Kenny had agreed to meet up that morning at 10 o'clock near the corner shop. This time they'd bring their bikes. Sadly Grandpa Jock said he just wanted to stay at home for a bit of a think.

George and Allison had definitely overheard the Ringmaster talking about the elephants going up to the new sanctuary, which was only a couple of miles away. It was worth a trip up there just to see what was going on.

George and Kenny arrived almost at the same time. Despite his unusual habits Kenny was quite a likeable lad and they fist bumped and stood straddling their bikes outside the little shop, occasionally shaking them from side to side.

'How's your little brother?' asked George, half out of politeness, half out of curiosity.

'Oh, the hospital thinks they found all the soldiers. But he has to go back for an x-ray today,' replied Kenny nonchalantly. To Kenny, there was nothing unusual about having objects removed from various nooks and crannies. It was the family hobby.

Kenny handed George a packet of cheese and onion crisps. George eyed them suspiciously, not sure where they might've been before.

'My mum gave us these for a snack,' said Kenny, beginning to open his packet.

'Eh, thanks,' replied George taking the crisps and checking that the bag was still sealed. He opened his packet and began stuffing the bag's contents into his mouth.

In between handfuls, Kenny suddenly blurted out, 'What's grey and highly dangerous?'

George smiled and said, 'I don't know, what is grey and highly dangerous?'

'An elephant with a machine gun!' Both boys began to snigger… this was going to get silly.

Kenny went on, 'What's big and grey and lives in a lake in Scotland?'

'I give up,' replied George.

'The Loch Ness Elephant!' And again both boys started to giggle but of course, they knew differently. There was the previous episode with Grandpa Jock's unidentified unsinkable underpants. George winked.

'A policeman runs up to a zookeeper and shouts "One of your elephants has been seen chasing a man on a bicycle." And the zookeeper replied "Nonsense, none of my elephants know how to ride a bicycle!"

'Boom, boom,' laughed George and Kenny sprayed a large mouthful of soggy crisps over the front of his bike. This made George snort and a little bit of snot shot out from one nostril.

Kenny closed his mouth and tried to hold back the rest of the crisps, which meant he joined George in snorting the contents out of his nose. The gooey snotter spat out a short way before twanging back and flopping down over Kenny's hand, which was covering his mouth.

The boys were now giggling uncontrollably and more snot and more crisps were being splattered everywhere. Without Allison's sensible girly influence, Kenny and George were regressing back to pre-school humour.

Right then, as if to bring a sense of order and discipline to the proceedings, Allison cycled up. The boys were still holding their sides laughing and wiping bogies and the crispy mush from their faces. Allison smiled at their nonsense and wanted to know what they found so funny.

'Here, get this,' said Kenny managing to control himself for a second. 'What's grey and goes round and round?'

Allison raised one eyebrow. George wasn't so sure. Allison smiled. 'I don't know, what is grey and goes round and round?'

'An elephant in a washing machine!' blurted out Kenny and started laughing again. George wasn't laughing though. He'd just seen Allison's face and she certainly wasn't laughing.

'Well, I don't think that's very funny, Kenny Roberts,' declared Allison, wiping the smile from Kenny's face. 'After thinking about those poor animals squashed into the back of a truck last night, the thought of an elephant squished into a washing machine is just not amusing in the least.'

'No, er, sorry,' mumbled Kenny, 'I just didn't think.' George quickly changed the subject.

'My Grandpa Jock was right though. There is something a bit suspicious about the circus.'

'Yes, those poor animals,' agreed Kenny, a little too eagerly, glancing at Allison. 'We should check out that sanctuary, just in case.' Allison looked at Kenny through slanted eyes and Kenny shuffled his feet nervously.

'Well, what are we waiting for?' urged George and he shot off down the hill towards the parade ground. Allison and Kenny kicked down on their pedals and gave chase, bouncing down the kerb and hurtling round the bend.

George was still in the lead by the time they'd reached the corner of the waste ground. Allison was close behind. Kenny was nowhere to be seen. On the corner opposite sat the pink and yellow box-shaped building called McDoball's.

'Don't suppose you fancy a burger, do you?' winked George.

'Ooh, no thanks,' choked Allison, 'I've had enough of burgers to last me a lifetime.'

'I'LL HAVE ONE!' shouted Kenny, now pedalling into view. He was still quite a way down the street, his cheeks were puffed out and again he was spraying crisps out of his mouth as he cycled.

'I'll have a burger,' he yelled as he got closer. 'Were you thinking about going in for a burger? I'll have one too.'

'Kenny, how can you think about burgers after eating that mush yesterday,' groaned George, his stomach turning at the prospect.

'I don't know,' replied Kenny. 'I must be more addicted to fast food than I thought.'

'You need to cut down then. You're awfully slow on that bike, Kenny.'

'I just didn't want to spill my crisps. That's all,' replied Kenny through another mouthful. 'Listen, just let me get a drink, OK. This cycling is thirsty work. ' And he dropped his bike and trotted off into the burger bar. He was back out again in a couple of minutes, slurping greedily on an extra-large cup of Power Pink.

'Ah, that's better,' he said, wiping his mouth with the back of his sleeve, 'I really could go a burger now though.' And he handed his drink to George, who was looking thirstily at it. George snatched the cup and began guzzling the juice up the straw.

'Seriously Kenny, have you learned nothing from eating that mulch yesterday?' moaned Allison.

'Actually,' said George, 'I'm feeling a bit peckish myself now too.'

'Not you as well, George? Give me that!' shrieked Allison and she snatched the big cup from George's hand. George made to grab it back desperately but Allison held him off at arm's length. She popped the lid with one hand and looked inside the container; a few cubes of melting ice and a little pink liquid swirling around at the bottom of the cup.

Dribbling out of the straw were tiny pieces of crisp. It did not look appetizing. Allison sniffed the drink.

It smelled sweet and sticky, like bubblegum and there was a fruity richness to it. Allison had to admit she felt her tummy rumble after the first couple of whiffs and that scared her. She threw the remaining contents down the nearest drain.

'Come on, you two. Let's go! We're not safe around here,' she yelled, picking up her bike.

'What do you mean,' asked George but Allison was pedalling furiously towards the parade ground and the boys were too stunned to do anything else but follow her. They cycled across the now-empty wasteland and onto the dirt track leading off around the back of the trees.

George and Kenny were struggling to keep up as Allison pedalled faster. They were now heading out of Little Pumpington and into the countryside beyond. There were trees, hedges and old stone walls lining both sides of the road and there were fields all around.

It was another two miles further up before Allison came to a halt. She threw her bike down and climbed over a dry-stone wall. She was still panting hard when George and Kenny plopped down next to her.

'What,' gasped George breathlessly, '....was....all.... that about?'

'Yeah,' wheezed Kenny. 'Not....safe.... from what?'

'From those burgers,' panted Allison. 'There's something in that drink that makes you want to eat burgers! And it even makes the burgers taste better.'

George scratched his head. He was aware of the almost over-powering rush he'd felt to scoff a burger almost as soon as he'd slurp up the Power Pink juice and George wasn't even as addicted to burgers as Crayon Kenny was.

'You're right,' agreed George finally, 'I see it now. I hated that thrown-together sawdust burger yesterday but still, I wanted to scoff another one as soon as I drunk that pink stuff today.'

'Where are we anyway?' asked Kenny, looking around deliberately, without wanting to admit his burger-cravings. He stared round at the rows of leafy green vegetables growing in the field.

'We're in a field,' suggested George helpfully.

'Well, d'uh!' exclaimed Kenny, 'I can see that. I meant what field? Where? And more importantly, Allison, Why?

'Why? Why do you think?' You were about to be taken over by burger brainwashing! I was getting us out of there,' yelled Allison defensively. 'And anyway, this is the elephant sanctuary!'

Chapter 13 - Trucks

Allison ordered the boys to stash the bikes and George noticed how much more bossy she was becoming, now that the welfare of the elephants might be at stake. She was really taking charge of things.

'We can come back for these later,' she said to no one in particular and she started marching off towards the gate. Kenny and George looked at each other and with resigned sighs, they trotted off behind her.

After a few minutes she said, 'What kind of vegetables are these, George? There're tons of them around here.'

'I think they're beetroots, 'replied George quickly.
'My Grandpa Jock used to grow beetroot in his garden. You can tell because of the red lines on the leaves.'

'Ooh, beetroot,' groaned Kenny. 'Messy.'

'Well, they would be if you stick them up your nose, Kenny.' Allison was still not amused by Crayon Kenny's antics.

'I don't think that I've ever stuck beetroot up my nose before,' mused Kenny, staring off into space with the little cogs in his head whirring hard. 'It's way too much trouble. I've eaten the pickled kind, out of a jar but the juice gets everywhere. It's really red, almost purple. It's kinda like blood.'

'You're being gross again, Kenny.' Allison screwed up her face and wrinkled her nose.

'It's true, Kenny's right,' said George and he quickly took out his little pocket screwdriver set and uprooted a small beetroot from the soil. His Grandpa Jock always carried a small screwdriver set too, in case of emergencies, and George had realised how useful they could be.

He flicked open the scissor section and cut beneath the outer skin of the dirty brown vegetable.

Beetroot juice oozed from the cut, dark red and thick. It coated his fingers and stained them pink.

'See,' said Kenny. 'It's really messy. My mum goes mental if I get it on my t-shirt cos it's really hard to get out.'

'My Grandpa Jock says they used the juice to dye clothes and flags in the olden days.' It was clear to see why. George held the beetroot up and his fingers were now covered in red stains and there was a trickle of crimson liquid running down his arm. 'He says it's even used to put extra red colour into tomato sauce!'

'There must be a good market for them then, because this farmer is growing millions!' exclaimed Allison, tired of George's vegetable lesson. She continued walking through the field and again, George and Kenny were forced to trot along behind as Allison's long strides stomped towards the road.

'The sign we saw from back there said 'Field 4' and that one says 'Field 6'. It points across the road.' Allison sounded confident that she knew what she was talking about, but the boys were still lost.

Allison turned around and her gaze followed the road down towards some farm buildings way off in the distance. A line of trees hid most of the view beyond that.

'Is that....?' Allison didn't finished what she was going to say. Kenny was too busy eating a bunch of beetroot leaves to notice. At least he wasn't sticking them anywhere he shouldn't. George followed Allison's gaze and he caught sight of movement too.

'Is that a truck?' he said.

It'sh coming thish way!' munched Kenny through a mouthful of leaves.

'HIDE!' yelled Allison and she dived into the nearest clump of beetroot plants. They were quite bushy and well formed and the ruts between the rows had been hollowed out by tractors' wheels so if Allison crouched low enough she was well hidden from the road. George and Kenny were quite used to following Allison's instructions by now and they jumped between the rows beside her.

'Maybe that's the elephants' truck again,' shouted Kenny, the noise of the big van almost drowning out any conversation. The diesel engine spluttered as it dropped a gear and slowly climbed the hill towards the gate.

'That's not the elephant truck. Look!' George was pointing between the leaves at the approaching vehicle. It was smaller, lighter in colour and had a logo across the side in big red letters. It read 'Relax, it's Fibre-Flush – Unblock That Log!'

The trio watched the truck drive passed. Above the slogan was a picture of a very relieved man sitting on a toilet. He was smiling and his eyes were slightly crossed in a comforting kind of way. He was definitely relaxed now.

'Fibre-Flush,' pointed Kenny, 'That's what they gave to my little brother in the hospital yesterday.'

'What?' exclaimed George and Allison together.

'Yeah, of course,' Kenny said casually. 'You can't expect doctors to root around in someone's bottom for too long, can you? Once they'd found the first few soldiers, a nurse gave him medicine to flush the rest of them out. I'm sure it was called Fibre-Flush.'

'So it's a laxative then,' said George. 'My Grandpa Jock says his bowels are bunged up sometimes and he needs a strong dose to get things moving again.'

'Too much information, George,' and Allison rolled her eyes.

'No, that happens to old people sometimes,' explained George. 'When he's constipated, he can't poo and needs a bit of help.'

'Oh right,' nodded Kenny. 'I think I must've had a laxalavvy thing too, at some point.'

'A laxative, Kenny. A laxative is a muscle relaxant for your bottom,' Allison explained. 'So, in your little brother's case he would expel any little toy soldiers that remained....' she shuddered, '...up there.'

'Oh yeah, I've definitely had that stuff then.'

'Let's not go there,' added Allison quickly.

'Doesn't half give you the bum's rush,' Kenny went on.

'No, stop.'

'You feel like your insides are being pushed out by a pneumatic drill.'

'Seriously, I mean it.'

'I had to sit on the toilet for an hour once. My legs were numb and I still didn't find that last marble.'

'ENOUGH!' yelled Allison, who was now red in the face.

'I was just saying,' shuffled Kenny. 'It really works well, at unblocking logs and bottoms and things.'

Allison wasn't listening. The gate had opened and the laxative truck had moved off towards the main road. Allison had just started to storm off in disgust when she trod in something round and mushy.

She stopped, lifted her foot and inspected the damage. The farmer must've have been muck spreading recently and there were still wet splodgy blobs of dung lying scattered between the rows of beetroots.

'That's just fertiliser,' said George quickly, hoping to make her feel better.

'Yeah,' sniggered Kenny, 'it's fresh, natural, organic fertiliser, from a horse, I think. You should be happy. At least it's none of that man-made stuff.'

Allison looked like she'd explode. 'I KNOW WHAT IT IS!'

'I'm not saying I'm an expert or anything.' replied Kenny.

'Here's a thought,' George had given up trying to lighten Allison's mood; she was way past placating. 'Horses, cows and deer all eat grass. Pretty much the same diet, right?'

'Right,' agreed Kenny, wondering where this was going.

'So, why are cows' poos big green squidgy pancakes, and horses' doo-dahs are tight round balls of poo and deer drop little pellets? They're all completely different.'

'I really don't know, George,' said Kenny, quite impressed.

'Well, don't talk to Allison about fertiliser when you don't know sh.....!'

'That's enough!' Allison quickly butted in but her face cracked and she finally smiled. 'You can't say that word, George. You're only ten.'

'I've heard way worse at school,' George laughed, 'but if it offends you, then I won't say it again.'

But Grandpa Jock would've been proud of that one, George thought and the three of them kept walking down through the muddy trench between the rows of beetroots. This time Allison was a little more careful where she put her feet.

'Why would an elephant sanctuary need laxatives?' wondered George aloud.

'Maybe the elephants need more fibre in their diet,' replied Allison, trying to be reasonable.

'TRUCKS!' shouted Kenny.

Once the laxative truck had left the farm property, the gate had stayed opened for a few extra seconds to allow seven dumper trucks to pull into the sanctuary and they were heading this way. Kenny, Allison and George dived for cover again, Allison still cautious about where she would land.

They peered out from between the beetroot leaves once more. The convoy of trucks whizzed passed them heading downhill towards the main block of buildings.

Each one was loaded full with fruit. The trucks were open-topped and the children could see pineapples, bananas, mangoes and apples piled high on the back. Occasionally when a truck bumped over a pot-hole, pieces of mushy fruit would fly out the back and splat on the road.

'That was a close one,' said George, as something narrowly missed Kenny's head.

'I didn't fancy getting squished by a mushy banana, mate,' groaned Kenny. Allison was now standing up looking at the rest of the fruit lying around.

'It's not the healthiest looking fruit I've ever seen before.' Allison was staring at the black bananas and over-ripe, almost rotting pineapples scattered across the tarmac. 'And I think the elephants must be getting enough fibre in their diet if that's what they're being fed.'

They followed the trucks in silence; Allison was rubbing her brow and George was scratching his head, both deep in thought. Kenny was picking his nose, the first knuckle of his forefinger deep in one nostril.

Chapter 14 – On Camera

Allison, George and Kenny walked down towards the main farmyard complex and just before the line of trees that sheltered the buildings from the fields there was a fork in the road. One path went off around to the rear of the complex; the other went straight into the heart of the buildings, in front of a big barn in the centre, next to a large swimming pool. There were what looked like offices to the right and a low, clinical building to the left was surrounded by a grassy park area.

One small van was parked at the edge of the complex but the fruit trucks were nowhere to be seen.

Allison waved at the boys to creep lower and they kept themselves hidden from view. As they crept closer they could hear music, happy, upbeat party music and at the edge of the trees George, Allison and Kenny peered out. The courtyard was a buzz of activity with a two-man television crew running all over the place, hauling their camera and boom microphone on their shoulders. There were dozens of elephants everywhere; they were having a brilliant time and the centre of the film crew's attention.

George could've sworn that some of the elephants were dancing, swinging their trunks in time to the music. Some of the elephants were swimming in the pool, adjacent to the barn. A few were spraying water from the pool over the other elephants. Some of the jumbos were munching into huge troughs of the juiciest, freshest fruit that had obviously come straight from the supermarket shelves. The apples had even been polished.

Other jumbos were playing football in the empty field with a large rubber ball and a few were casually standing off to the side with wooden easels in front of them. They were actually holding paint brushes delicately with their trunks whilst painting scenic landscape pictures. If it was possible for elephants to smile, these elephants would be beaming from ear to ear with delight.

'They're having a party,' whispered Kenny.

'They're painting,' added George.

'They're certainly being looked after very well,' gasped Allison. 'And they seem to be having a good time too.'

George glanced over to Allison and he thought she looked a little disappointed, hoping she could be the one to free the elephants from an evil captivity. Yet, it wasn't evil at all.

Fortunately for the elephants, they were having a ball. They had the freedom of the fields, the delight of the courtyard; they had an abundance of fruit to eat and a large swimming pool to splash around in.

The film crew followed the elephants around, pointing their camera at their antics and lapping up their enjoyment in their new sanctuary.

George noticed that over in the corner there stood one man with headphones on and a clipboard in his arms. He looked like he was the TV director because he kept shouting instructions to the TV crew.

Allison nudged George and pointed over the centre of the compound. Across at the barn the two huge sliding doors were almost shut. There was however, a small gap with just enough space for three heads to poke their way around.

Ronald the Ringmaster and the two chimps were standing discreetly inside the barn. George could only see the Ringmaster's head so he couldn't tell if he was still thin or had rediscovered his big belly. And talking of bellies, George couldn't see their circus elephants anywhere; lots of other elephants but Nelly, Smelly, Delhi and Jelly were nowhere to be seen.

Allison whispered, 'Come on, I want to hear what's going on.' And she crept closer to the main building.

George and Kenny had no choice but to follow her again. Allison came to a stop at the edge of the courtyard, right on the corner of the low block building and behind a gigantic wheelbarrow filled luscious fruit. The director with the clipboard stepped towards his film crew, one man carrying a camera and the other holding what looked like a large fluffy sausage on the end of a stick.

'That's a microphone,' whispered Allison.

'I know that,' said Kenny sharply. 'And that's the camera, I'm not thick, you know.'

'And that's them leaving,' pointed George, as the TV director, the cameraman and the sound engineer hopped into the small van and sped off up the road.

Chapter 15 – Press Release

McDOBALLS

The McDoballs Corporation

Press Release – Announcement to the Media

The McDoballs Corporation is proud to announce the opening of Britain's very first Elephant Sanctuary!

With changes in government legislation regarding the housing and treatment of these magnificent creatures, and the fact that they will never be allowed to perform again as live, animal entertainment, there was a threat to the dozens of elephants currently living in the country. We, at McDoballs, could not stand idly by and see the slaughter of the largest land mammals on the planet.

So, McDoballs have created a charitable organisation called EAZY PEEZEE.org to protect these elephants, providing a unique, state-of-the-art facility in the north-east of England. This project will allow these fine animals, who have lived a hard life for our pleasure, enjoyment and entertainment, to want for nothing. Their meals will be provided through exquisite dining, on the freshest most delicious fruits and roots that money can buy. They can play, they can paint, and they can swim. Their every whim is catered for.

You will see from our public information film that this sanctuary is a place of tranquillity for these wondrous beasts, where they can live out the rest of their days in

*safety and harmony, never having to perform tricks
again, never forced to live in cramped, confined
conditions ever again.*

*These poor creatures have been subject to the public's
cruel gaze long enough. We must allow them peace and
quiet, if they are to forgive us for the life we have forced
them to lead in the name of entertainment.*

*The benevolence of the McDoballs Corporation asks for
nothing in return, apart from the heartfelt joy it gives to
provide the care and consideration for our new guests,
and to install reassurance and love in their minds and in
their hearts.*

*Our only wish is that these magnificent creatures are left
in peace, alone and discreetly isolated from us all. Their
seclusion is their salvation. Please allow these noble animals
the privacy of their much-deserved isolation.*

Thank you

End of message

I'M STUFFIN' IT

Chapter 16 – Email 3

From: *Head of Marketing*
To: *Chief Operating Officer*
Cc: *All other Department Executives*
Subject: Manipulation Campaign for Product X

Dear all

The latest part of our media manipulation campaign has been successful. The film crew were in attendance at the 'sanctuary' today and we were able to demonstrate the facilities in a most favourable light.

Our press release and news broadcast went out online and to all the British and world newspapers on time. It was shown across all media channels and reported in every newspaper in the UK.

The media coverage was unanimously supportive of our new charity initiative and public reaction has been overwhelmingly positive. Opinion polls suggest that consumers do not want the animals to be disturbed and it is recommended we push on with Project X with no more unwanted interruptions.

Our new operations director is overseeing activities at the production centre and our charity's executive directors are now in their rightful place. Ultimately, these two directors will take overall responsibility for the production of Product X, and if the truth ever comes to light, we will be able to maintain corporate ignorance and plausible deniability.

The truth cannot be traced back to the McDoballs Corporation.

Thank you
B.S. Woffel

Chapter 17– Our Elephants Appear

George stared across at the barn again. Ronald the Ringmaster, complete with his large-again belly, tight black dungarees and smart pink boots, snapped his fingers and disappeared back inside with Pippo and Zippy. Only the elephants remained to enjoy the courtyard but it wasn't long before the peace was shattered by a series of bangs and clatters emanating from inside the barn.

Suddenly the sliding doors began to roll open and the two chimps reappeared to push them the last little way. The barn was fully exposed and from the darkness there came a great roar of a diesel engine, a cloud of blue smoke and a truck reversed out towing a massive cage.

'Surely those poor circus elephants haven't been cooped up in that cage all night?' gasped Allison.

But as the truck reversed further, it was obvious that the elephants were still in there, as the large grey body of Smelly the elephant was squashed up against the bars of the cage and squished flesh was oozing from within the tight cubicle.

Pippo pulled the ramp down until it bumped against the ground. Zippy hopped up to the cage and unlocked the giant padlock, swinging the door slowly around. Part of Smelly's body plopped out of the cage but the fat elephant was having difficulty removing herself from the mass of bodies inside. George realised that the elephants had been squished so hard overnight they had almost merged together, like squashing lumps of clay in a giant jumbo mould.

With a wrench Smelly pulled herself free and her tummy began to expand to its normal girth again. The elephant's eyes were dark and heavy, her trunk drooped and she wore a sad expression across her wrinkled face. Next out was Delhi, her trunk lifting to suck in lungfuls of clean, fresh air.

After all, her head had been pressed into Smelly's bottom all night.

Next to exit was Nelly, the mother of the herd and the proudest elephant George had ever seen. Eighteen hours in a cramped cage hadn't crushed her spirit and her eyes defiantly scanned her new surroundings, checking on her companions and narrowing slightly at the sight of Pippo and Zippy standing at either side of the ramp.

Nelly walked between the two chimps to where the rest of the herd had gathered. Other elephants had noticed the new arrivals and were gathering round, reassuring and welcoming their guests. Trunks were linked. Soft, low trumpet calls whispered between the animals and there was a gentle nuzzling of big bodies, ears and noses.

Nelly stood at the bottom on the ramp, waiting patiently.

Finally, last out of the cage, slowly at first, blinking and unsteady, the smallest elephant appeared. Jelly the baby elephant had been put in first in, perhaps to lure Nelly in, and was last to emerge. The little calf, with eyes big and brown, was visibly smaller and definitely thinner. Three elephants squashed on top of you all night would do that.

A steadying trunk came out from Nelly as Jelly started to make her way down the ramp. The rest of the elephants separated at the bottom and formed a pathway for the little jumbo to follow, as kind trunks supported the little elephant's wavering steps.

George sneaked a glance over at Allison, who was quietly wiping away a tear. Even Crayon Kenny had the good grace to stop picking his nose for a few moments and watch the tender tale unfold. As mighty and majestic as the elephants were, it was clear to see how important their extended family was.

Once at the bottom, Jelly's trunk began to twitch and the hungry baby jumbo staggered over to the first barrow of fruit that had been laid out for the television cameras. Gentle caresses came from all directions as Jelly lifted up a bright red apple from the barrow with her trunk and popped it into her mouth.

The wonderful, sweet juice had an invigorating effect and Jelly began to liven immediately. The first apple was followed by a second, then a third. The other freed elephants joined Jelly in their first meal of the day.

Kenny rubbed his eyes. 'It's just sand or something,' he insisted.' I've got grit in my eye.'

George and Allison just smiled.

They watched quietly for a while as the elephants ate their fill. Then Delhi walked over to one of the elephants standing beside an easel and with great curiosity, she watched as her new jumbo friend gently took up a paintbrush in her trunk and began to gracefully stroke the bristles across the canvas.

George saw a picture emerge of an elephant holding a flower in its trunk. 'It's like a welcoming present,' he thought.

Nelly continued to look on, perhaps in puzzlement at first, then allowing the brief memory of an elephant's paradise to cross her mind. Were these the luxuries that the Ringmaster had promised?

'Come on,' whispered Allison, 'I think we've seen enough.'

'Not yet,' hissed George and he ran from behind the barrow of fruit and dashed over to the window of the low block building. It was painted white, it looked clinical and efficient and there was just enough space left at the bottom of blinds for George to see what was inside. He peered through the glass for a few seconds.

Kenny and Allison ran from behind the fruit barrows, crossed around the edge of the courtyard and up again towards the trees, still crouching. George caught up with them again at the corner of the beetroot fields, keeping low and hidden amongst the leaves.

'What did you see in there?' asked Kenny.

'Nothing much,' replied George. 'That looks like a laboratory in there, with test-tubes and syringes and things.'

'I guess we were wrong about all this,' said Allison.

'But what about the fat-thin-fat Ringmaster guy? That's not just crash dieting, you know,' puzzled Kenny.

'I suppose it was dark last night, and maybe we didn't really see him properly.' George was now trying to convince himself.

'One thing still bothers me though. Why were the elephants kept squashed in that cage over night?' wondered Allison.

'Who knows?' shrugged Kenny. 'The elephants were certainly enjoying themselves this morning.'

'Let's go tell my Grandpa there's no mystery here,' nodded George. 'Just a playground paradise for unemployed elephants.'

Chapter 18 – Journey Home

It took them much longer to cycle back from the elephant sanctuary than it did to get out there, mainly because they spent twenty minutes pulling Kenny away from the windows at McDoballs. He'd been lured in by the wafting smell of cooking fat and chips.

'Just the one. Just one burger!' he kept shouting as he practically forced his face up against the glass.

George and Allison tried taking an arm each to pull him away but Kenny was so desperate that at one point he jerked forward, causing George and Allison to lose their grip of him and Kenny smashed his face against the glass. The burger bar was full of customers, who were all staring at the menu board behind the counter but none of them heard the loud bang on the window. They were too intent on getting their burger fix.

The bump to the head didn't stop Kenny's desire for a burger either. So much so, he started to lick the poster of a big Bagel Burger that was on the inside.

'Er, Kenny,' pointed out Allison in disgust, 'you're licking the dirt off the windows now.'

'I'd hate to think what would happen if he found a thrown-away burger in the gutter,' groaned George, still pulling at Kenny's arms. 'Eat it up from the ground, probably.'

'That's what I've noticed,' replied Allison, yanking Kenny backwards, 'no-one seems to throw away their burgers. There's a lot of litter scattered around but not much wasted food.'

'Thath's becauth they tho tasthy,' mushed Kenny, his tongue pressed against the glass and a long trail of drool was running down the window.

Eventually the only way for George and Allison to prize Kenny away from the vicinity of the burger bar was when

Allison ran round to the drive-in section, swiped a large cup of Power Pink from the serving window and threw a couple of pound coins on the counter.

'It's an emergency!' she shouted and the bored, vacant expression of the pimply youth in the take-away booth seemed to suggest that he experienced those types of emergencies a lot.

Allison wafted the cup in front of Kenny's face and he soon forgot about licking the glass. Allison was already on her bike and she sped off up the hill. George was only able to hold Kenny back for a few seconds to give Allison a head start before Kenny pulled free, jumped on his bike and gave chase, still dribbling. George hopped on his bike and joined the mad procession.

By the time George caught up with his two friends, just past the little newsagent shop Kenny was lying on his back on the pavement, holding his bulging belly with an empty juice carton rolling around on the ground beside him.

'He drank the whole lot,' gasped Allison trying to catch her breath, 'in one gulp!'

'He must've been thirsty,' replied George.

'He must be greedy, you mean.' Allison rolled her eyes and turned to see a panting, gulping Kenny trying to lean forward, still holding his tummy...

BUUUUUURRRRRRRRRRRRRRRRRRRRRRRPPP!

'Well done, mate... that was a ripper!' said George with some admiration.

'You two are absolutely disgusting. I don't know why I'm hanging out with you,' fumed Allison. 'I bought you that Power Pink juice thing to get you away from McDoballs,' she went on, 'and all you can do is belch like a buffalo.'

'I'm sorry. I couldn't help it,' wheezed Kenny.

'That's no excuse for burping like a bull,' Allison went on.

'No, I mean I couldn't help drinking all that stuff at once.'

'It's like the juice had a mad grip on me,' exclaimed Kenny, looking for some sympathy. Allison raised an eyebrow.

'Well, we did say that that stuff was addictive,' shrugged George. 'I think that just about proves it now.'

'Actually, you might have a point,' admitted Allison.

'Actually, I think I might be sick,' groaned Kenny, turning a delicate shade of green.

'I knew he shouldn't have drunk all that juice so fast.'

George felt he had to step in a help his queasy friend. 'Come on then, let's get him home. He only lives round the corner.'

George put his arm round his mate's shoulder and they staggered off towards the end of the road.

The second house down was a large grey bricked building. There was a low wall surrounding a neatly cut lawn and a flower border. In the corner of the garden was a small boy, crouching in the dirt.

'That's my little brother,' groaned Kenny, still quite pale.

'What's he doing down there?' asked George.

'I'm playing with my soldiers,' smiled the little boy. A dozen plastic soldiers were scattered around the flower beds.

'What soldiers?' yakked George.

'Not *the* soldiers?' choked Allison.

'Probably,' nodded George.

'The doctor says they're all clean now,' giggled the little boy and as if to prove the point, he licked one.

'Oh stop it,' moaned Allison, 'you don't know where they've been.'

'Yes I do,' the boy replied smartly. 'They've been up my.......'

'ENOUGH! Get Kenny inside, George,' yelled Allison, trying to drown out the small boy's words. 'I'll put his bike in the garage.'

By the time George came out of the house Allison was standing on the opposite side of the road. George shut the gate behind him, picked up his bike and crossed over.

'I couldn't bear the sight of that little boy, licking his soldiers like that.' Allison shuddered.

'Yeah, strange kid,' agreed George.

'Strange? He's weird!' Allison paused. 'Just like his big brother.'

'But it's strange how addicted Kenny was to that juice though?' added George. 'Do you think they put something in it?'

'It would be a great way to keep customers coming back, wouldn't it?' said Allison, now believing that George could be right.

Then she stopped. 'George, can you hear sirens?' Allison turned and saw a figure way off in the distance gliding towards them. George saw it too.

'What's that?' asked Allison.

'Looks like an old woman on a skateboard,' suggested George. As 'she' approached, he could see a shock of ginger hair blowing around on top of the figure's head and her skirt was flapping wildly in the breeze.

'But she's bald on top? A bald old woman?' quizzed Allison, 'with a moustache?'

'Actually, it's not a skateboard. It's a scooter,' peered George, and then he paused. 'That's my scooter!'

'What's a bald old woman with a ginger moustache doing riding your scooter?' puzzled Allison. 'And if that skirt blows up any higher, we'll see what she had for breakfast!'

'That's not a skirt,' smiled George, 'that's a kilt.'

'That's your Grandpa Jock!' gasped Allison, now realising that the tartan terror wheeling closer was actually the mad old Scotsman, the hair around his ears blowing madly as the scooter sped faster.

'Yup, wearing his Sunday best and it's the middle of the week,' said George, laying down his bike. 'And those sirens are getting louder!'

'Er, George? He's not slowing down, George,' Allison's bottom lip quivered as she spoke. 'He's getting faster, George. Why doesn't he use the brake?'

Grandpa Jock shot across the road without even looking; reckless, thought George as his grandfather's eyeballs nearly popped out of his head. He'd skilfully negotiated the first kerb but the uphill bump on the other side was fast approaching. He bent his legs and pulled up on the handle bars precisely at the right moment.

That is, if he precisely meant to clip the centre of the foot-plate against the kerb. Grandpa Jock flew forwards, arms, legs, scooter and kilt all flying off in different directions.

The scooter crashed to the ground. Grandpa Jock seemed to hover in mid-air for a split second longer before landing feet first, knees next, then hands, elbows, head tucked into a forward roll and finally onto his feet again.

There was a pause and George was about to burst into applause for a perfect dismount. Sadly, the 'oomph' in his old knees failed to boost the Scotsman back on to his feet. Grandpa Jock slowly rolled backwards and flopped onto the ground, arms spread wide.

He lay there panting; his face red from his exertions, his hands were stained pink and his long fingernails had thick purple muck caked underneath them.

'I'm glad to see you, Grandpa but what's the hurry?' asked George.

'I'm just glad you put pants on,' admitted Allison, averting her eyes.

'It's....easy........,' gasped Grandpa Jock, breathless from his exertions.

'You didn't make it look easy, Grandpa.' George was

rolling his eyes. 'You actually made it look quite tricky. You nearly landed on your face!'

'Naw, naw, it's....' Grandpa Jock was still fighting for breath, '....it's Eazy-Peezee!'

Chapter 19 – Monkey Business!

'Yeah, Grandpa. Easy-peasy-lemon-squeezy but you still nearly landed face first on the pavement.' George was shaking his head.

'Why didn't you use your brake, Mr Jock?' asked Allison.

'Naw, I mean Eazy.....' Grandpa Jock stopped abruptly and stared at Allison. 'What, you mean these things have brakes?'

'Yes, of course,' giggled Allison.' Didn't you know? It's the little fender bar at the back. You just press down with your foot.'

'Well, they didn't have brakes on scooters in my day!' mumbled Grandpa Jock, feeling slightly sheepish.

'But what are you doing on my scooter, apart from somersaults, mad acrobatics and basically falling off?' George wrinkled his nose up, as the sirens got louder still. 'And you're not being chased by the police, are you?'

'Oh yeah, I'd better be quick,' chortled Grandpa Jock. 'They think I'm mad and they're going to lock me up.'

'You're not that mad, Grandpa. Not yet.' George's voice was unsteady, as he thought of the consequences. Grandpa Jock just winked at Allison.

'I've just seen something about yon elephant sanctuary..... on Face Tube, or something,' he went on. 'There was a report about the Eazy PeeZee.org elephant charity so I did a wee bit o' checking on the internet thingy, didn't I?'

Grandpa Jock narrowed his eyes, drawing the children in closer.

'And I finally discovered a website called The Company House, an official government website where every company in the country needs to register their business interests.'

'And?' George and Allison were hanging on his every word.

'The Eazy-PeeZee......'

'Yes?'

'dot org...'

'Yes?!'

'......elephant charity.....'

'COME ON!' George was sure he'd burst.

'...was set up just a few short months ago and has only two directors......' revealed Grandpa Jock, his eyes twinkling.

'Is that it?' blurted out George, more than a little disappointed.

'Those two directors are......' Grandpa Jock paused again, trying to build up the suspense again. George didn't want to fall for it a second time.

'Pippo and Zippy!' declared Grandpa Jock proudly.

'The circus chimps?! No way!'

'Yes, way!' announced Grandpa Jock triumphantly. 'The very same. I've been suspicious about their monkey business for some time now.'

'I told you that's why you called them 'cunning little business monkeys' said George.

'I've been doing some digging into their activities for a while, especially after someone named their circus after them for tax reasons,' Grandpa Jock was becoming all conspiratorial again. 'But once I heard about the Eazy-Peezee wotsit thingy, it all fell into place.' Grandpa Jock was ready to take a bow but George and Allison were still not getting it.

'What on earth are you talking about, Grandpa?' gawped George.

'I'll start at the beginning, shall I?' Grandpa Jock went on, rolling his eyes at density of the modern generation.

'A few years back, somebody realised how easy it was to create a company with animals on the board of directors.

I think the first company to do it used a mouse and a duck.' Grandpa Jock grinned.

'Anyway, if your chief executive or managing director was an animal then that company didn't have to pay as much tax. There's a bit of a loophole in the law that lets those companies be treated more like charities.' Grandpa Jock was enjoying his moment.

'So, Pippo and Zippy's Amazing Animal Circus was set up with them in charge?' asked George, beginning to catch on.

'Yes,' gasped Grandpa Jock. 'The company can avoid paying tax and it's the executive chimps who take the blame if anything goes wrong!'

'But that's not the best of it,' said Grandpa Jock, saving the good bit till last. 'Pippo and Zippy would appear to be, according to The Company House archives, the top directors in a another five companies, including the circus.' Grandpa Jock was growing impatient, as the screaming sirens grew louder.

'Chimps can't be in charge of businesses!' exclaimed George.

'What are the other companies, Mr Jock?' asked Allison, realising he might be onto something.

'Well, apart from the Eazy-PeeZee.org and the circus, they are also the joint managing directors of Eazy-PeeZee Cheese Ltd, who seem to be into food manufacturing.' George and Allison's eyes widened as Grandpa Jock went on...

'They also head up Eazy-PeeZee Treeze Ltd, which is some kind of timber company in Scotland. And last, but by no means least, Eazy PeeZee Squeezy Ltd, a laxative manufacturer and wholesale buyer of rotten fruit!'

'Rotten fruit!' declared George. 'We saw all that rotten fruit being delivered up to the elephants. Maybe they squeeze the juice out of the fruit first.'

'And that laxative van!' Allison gasped. It all made sense now...in a far-fetched, ridiculous kind of way.

But it was too late. An ambulance and a police car had screeched to a halt at the side of the kerb. A sergeant, a constable and two paramedics had jumped out and ran round to where Grandpa Jock had landed. The officers grabbed the old Scotsman by the shoulders, whilst one of the paramedics shoved a syringe into his arm.

'That should calm him down a bit,' laughed one of the policemen. 'He'll not give us the slip again.'

'Wait!' shouted George. 'What are you doing with my grandpa?'

'It's for his own safety,' smiled the older paramedic sympathetically. 'We think your grandpa's mentally unsound. He was seen digging around in elephant poo on the waste-ground and someone called the police. Apparently he was playing with the stuff.'

'Right, but don't worry. We just need to check him out... do some tests, you know,' agreed the other paramedic.

'Maybe they'll lock the mad old duffer up for good this time,' snapped the police sergeant. 'We've been chasing him around Little Pumpington for miles.'

Grandpa Jock had slumped on the ground, dribbling, as the drugs kicked in. The two police officers dragged him to the back of the ambulance and unceremoniously dumped him inside, handcuffing him to the trolley.

The shock hit George and his mouth drooped open. He was still speechless when the ambulance drove around the corner and disappeared out of sight.

Chapter 20 – The Camera Never Lies

George woke up late the following morning. Yesterday had been a tiring one; the bike rides, burger fights, sneaking around beetroot fields, practically dragging his barf-buddy Kenny back home and then the shock of watching his grandfather being taken away to a mental institution.

He was slumped down on the sofa watching cartoons and he hadn't even heard Allison come in.

'Hey,' said Allison softly. George nearly filled his pants.

'ALLISON! YOU FREAK!' screamed George. 'You can't sneak up on people like that.'

'Ok, ok, chill out,' she giggled. 'I met your mum outside. She said go straight in.'

'What? To give her only son a heart attack?'

'Oh, stop being so melodramatic, George,' she smiled, her eyebrows bobbing up and down. 'Neat jim-jams, by the way'

George realised that he was still wearing his pyjamas... the ones with the little rockets on them!

'Oh, these. They're not little kid pyjamas, they're...um... retro. Yeah, like ironic.' George thought that Allison's smile might've turned a little sarcastic so he gave up trying to sound cool. He couldn't pull it off properly.

'Haven't you seen the news yet?' Allison asked, politely changing the subject.

'I've been a bit pre-occupied, alright.' George moaned. 'My Grandpa Jock was locked up for being a nutcase, in case you hadn't noticed.'

'You should watch the news.' Allison's eyes flickered with pride. 'Someone you might recognise?'

'Who?' snapped George.

'Just watch it, will you?' Allison wanted her secret to hit George in the face like a giant cartoon frying pan and she grabbed the remote control.

'Any news channel will do,' she said, flicking the buttons. 'It's been on around the clock, and they're all pretty much the same.'

Allison took a few seconds to find a news channel. An elephant appeared, painting on a canvas.

'These majestic creatures,' said the newscaster, 'have finally found sanctuary in the most unlikely of places. Born in captivity, following generations accustomed to the wild savannahs of Africa, these mighty pachyderms have discovered peace and tranquillity in the north of England.'

'Yeah, Little Pumpington.' George was nodding furiously.

'Be quiet, George. Here it comes!' Allison was getting tense now too.

'...who have lived a hard life for our pleasure, enjoyment and entertainment,' the reporter went on, as the camera panned back, opening out to wider shot of the barn behind the elephants. This is what Allison had been waiting for.

George watched the screen. Just up in the corner, a fat man in pink boots was pulling a large pillow out from his black dungarees. Instantly the man transformed from a bulging size 50inch waist to a slim 32".

'Recognise him?' Allison raised one eyebrow.

The man's dungarees had become baggy and saggy and flopped around his thin frame. The camera began to focus in on the panoramic scenery behind the barn, shifting away from the building. Allison hit the pause button.

As the scene had zoomed in on the scenery beyond, a man in the pink boots was caught by the camera, closer if a little fuzzier.

'Who's that then?' asked Allison again.

'No idea,' replied George, pushing out his bottom lip and shaking his head.

'Look closer,' urged Allison, pointing at the television screen.

'Er....the ringmaster guy?' George was clutching at straws.

'It's Mr Jolly!' screeched Allison.

'Mr Jolly the janitor?' squealed George, in a voice way too high pitched to sound cool. 'Er, I mean Mr Jolly the janitor?' he said again in a gruff manly baritone.

'Yes!' urged Allison.

'Our old janitor?' George was still puzzled.

'YES!' Now Allison was ready to burst.

'Nah, can't be,' dismissed George.

'Why not?' gasped Allison, 'Look at his hair, his eyes, his pink wellies, ignore the moustache. I knew I'd seen him before.'

George had to agree, there was something familiar about Ronald the Ringmaster.

'But our janitor's dead, isn't he?' mused George. 'He was blown up in that explosion at the school.'

'But the police didn't find a body,' Allison went on, 'They only found a pair of pink wellington boots, slightly scorched around the edges. But no proof he was actually a goner.'

'Mr Jolly?' mused George, '....the janitor......is now....... Ronald the Ringmaster?'

'What's so different about those two jobs anyway?' Allison was forcing her point of view across now, 'You always said Mr Jolly called the children at the school a bunch of animals. Clearing up after school kids? Clearing up after animals in a circus? Basically the same, isn't it'

'Big school kids don't usually poo everywhere,' argued George. 'Mind you, the little ones might... if their poo was pink,' he giggled.

The pause button was holding Ronald the Ringmaster still, with a pillow in his hand and two chimpanzees at his feet. George stared at the TV screen for a few more seconds before a thought thunderbolt struck him square between the eyes.

'Grab the bikes, Allison,' he yelled.

Chapter 21 – Catch of the Day!

Forty minutes later Allison and George were defying the television appeal to give the elephants some well-deserved privacy and crawling along behind the trees at the edge of the sanctuary complex. Their bikes were hidden in the beetroot fields again.

However, instead of fruit trucks and a laxative lorry, this time they had to hide from several large tankers driving out from the farm.

'Are they petrol tankers?' Allison asked.

'I don't know what they're for,' replied George. 'There's no logo on them. They're not even marked with chemical warning stickers. Who knows what's inside?'

The courtyard was empty. There were no elephants playing football, no elephants painting or swimming or splashing about. The doors to the barn were closed and all the blinds were pulled shut on the laboratory and the office was in darkness. There was a low muffled hum of an engine.

'Where's everybody gone?' said Allison.

'Maybe they're all off for a walk, you know, stretching their legs,' suggested George. 'It's a big place.'

Then George smiled, 'or maybe they've gone to unpack their trunks?'

Allison shook her head. 'What are all those pipes and big tubes doing in the swimming pool?'

'Maybe they're for cleaning the water out,' replied George, deciding to stand on his tip toes to get a better look. 'The tubes are coming from the laboratory.'

'Get down!' Allison yelled, pulling at George's belt, 'Somebody will see you.'

'Never mind seeing me, you need to look at this.' George turned to Allison with his eyes wide. Allison stood up but pressed herself closer to the tree for cover.

The water in the swimming pool was pink. Not just a hint of pink or a delicate rosé shade but a rich, bold, almost shocking pink colour that sparkled in the sunlight.

'A pink pool?' gasped Allison.

'For pink elephants?' George could only shrug his shoulders.

'Let's get a closer look. There must be another way in round the back.' Allison pulled George's arm and they crept around the edge of the buildings. There was a slight breeze blowing but George was sure he could smell a musty, grassy aroma. He kept sniffing all the way around the back of the barn. This smell was getting stronger.

At the back of the barn there was a metal staircase leading up to a door at the top. There was a sign across the top that read 'Fire Exit'.

'Let's try up there.' and they both climbed the steps. At the top, the door was slightly open. Allison slipped her fingers into the crack and pulled the door wide. They stepped into the darkness.

Immediately George and Allison were hit by a warm wave of elephant odour, like baking hay, which hung heavily in the air. Allison's eyes started to water but after that, a fruitier smell followed. Once they'd been blown over by the initial overpowering stench, it was replaced by a strange sweetness; an earthy, bubblegum bouquet and George began to inhale deeply.

'That's quite nice, once you get used to it,' he said. The noise of the engine was louder in here and George's eyes were adjusting to the light. Allison stepped on ahead, holding her hands out in front. They walked carefully along together, hoping to make out some familiar shapes. The warm, burnt cherry perfume wrapped around them like candy floss.

BANG!

Behind them, the exit door slammed shut and blocked out any light they had. It was now pitch black.

'Must've been the wind,' they both said together, neither sounding convinced.

They turned and shuffled their way through the darkness back to the door. Allison reached out for the handle and she rattled it back and forth.

'It's locked,' she said started to panic. She twisted the handle faster.

'It can't be,' replied George, taking her hand and shaking the doorknob harder. They stopped.

Behind them, from the heart of the barn came a long, low rumble. A soft moaning joined in and finally a deafening trumpet blast made both George and Allison cover their ears. More trumpets joined in, in a cacophony of sound.

FLASH!

The blackness of dark was instantly replaced by the blindness of bright, white light. At first, George and Allison held their eyelids tight shut until the flashes began to clear in their heads but soon they began to blink. Three rows of fluorescent tubes were now illuminating the barn.

They were high up on a first floor gantry, the roof of the barn above. Running down the centre was a long wooden corridor that sloped gently downwards away from them. At the end of this corridor, the floor dropped off sharply. On either side of this corridor were rows of metal cages. There were two smaller, narrower pathways behind the cages and inside each metal cage was a squashed elephant.

George and Allison began to walk down between the cages. The elephants were crammed so tightly in that the bars pressed into their skin. The elephants were actually bursting out; looking as if they'd explode at any minute.

There was a long trough in front of each cage filled with mushy bananas, pineapples, other fruits and loads and loads of beetroots. Dozens of the crimson vegetables were stacked into every feeding tray and red beetroot juice dripped and stained onto the floor. None of the elephants were eating.

At first, there was just a little squeak. Then a parp and a pump. A short poop, then a long trumpet blast. The air was filling again with a warm ripe aroma of that earthy sweetness, as every elephant blew off the contents of their bowels. The rumbling didn't stop.

Blast! Parp! Pump! Dump! Splodge!

As this farting, blasting concerto squirted and squidged its way to another level, Allison tried to cover her eyes, ears and nose all at the same time. George knew there was no escaping the sights, sound and smells so he decided he wanted a closer look.

He ran round behind the row of cages to check his suspicions. Every elephant had lifted their tail and big crimson balls of dung were dolloping out of each enormous bottom, dumping out piles of pink poo.

Another trough ran along the back of the cages, catching every animal's excretions and a small jet of water hosed and flushed the pink poo downhill along to the end. George hoped that none of the elephants pushed too hard as he edged along this back passageway. He didn't want to be pebble-dashed in pink so he kept moving, too frightened to stay in one place too long.

At last, with an aromatic finale, the pumping and dumping came to an exhausted end.

At the bottom of the sloping trough the jumbos' giant jobbies were being harvested in a massive, round mixing tank. This huge vat was sitting on the ground floor below and looked about three metres deep.

The dung was flowing into it from both sides and two huge blades were churning, slicing, mashing and folding the poop together. The jet of water flushing the poo into the vat was turning the dollops of pink poop into mushy, fibrous, pink custard.

The mechanical noise that George had heard earlier was the engine driving the blades around like an electric food blender. A pump was forcing the pulped poop into a pipe and pushing it outside through a gap in the wall. George ran round the front again to the central corridor.

Once the elephants had stopped dumping, they actually looked thinner, which wasn't surprising since they'd each just cranked out a couple of hundred kilos of crimson crap. And now they were feeling empty again, the elephants started eating automatically; munching into the fruit and beetroots as if they hadn't seen food for a month.

Allison stood in the very centre of the corridor. 'You look a bit shell-shocked,' said George,

'It's not easy to take all this in,' replied Allison.

'Well, except the smell perhaps,' George offered, 'it's quite easy to take that in.'

But realising that this wasn't the time for humour, he walked up to his friend and put his hand on her shoulder.

'You're not going to believe this....' George began but before he could finish a large net dropped from the ceiling and engulfed the two of them. Their fingers became twisted and entwined in the strings and the more they struggled, the more entangled they became. George stumbled as the net wrapped round his feet. He toppled over, pulling Allison down with him.

They couldn't move their feet. They felt their ankles bound together and they lay there helpless, like a couple of codfish. George tried to look down but he couldn't move his head further than Allison's shoulder. Allison could just make out a couple of hairy heads bouncing about beneath her feet.

A familiar voice boomed from above.

'Bravo! Ladies and gentlemen, I give you....The catch of the day!'

Chapter 22 – Pink Poo Revealed

'Hoist away!'

George and Allison felt themselves being dragged by their feet and then lifted upside down into the air in the net. As he swung backwards George could make out two chimpanzees cranking a large handle that was attached to the rope. The rope was bound to their ankles, suspending them in mid-air linked through a pulley in the ceiling. The harder the chimps cranked, the higher George and Allison went up.

Pippo finally locked the crank handle, and George and Allison swung gently back and forth. Zippy chattered loudly with excitement. Ronald the Ringmaster strode down the corridor. Pippo and Zippy jumped back to allow him to march past. He walked around the dangling bag of children, eyeing them with a malicious sneer.

'We've been expecting you,' he hissed. 'Thought nobody could see you behind that fruit barrow, did you? Thought you could hide out of sight. You've caused me enough trouble to last two lifetimes. Well, that ends now.'

George was trapped and upside down but he hadn't lost his voice. He wouldn't allow a little thing like gravity stop him from saying what was on his mind.

'Nice to see you again, Mr Jolly!'

'I wondered when someone would notice,' the Ringmaster shrugged. 'Coming back to Little Pumpington was always a risk.'

'So you are our old janitor,' Allison gasped. 'We thought you'd been blown up with our school.'

'Everybody thought I was blown up with the school. I just used that to my advantage.' Ronald kept walking around the swinging net, twisting the riding crop he held in his hand.

'It was the pink boots that gave it away,' said George.

'And the big cushion shoved down the front of your trousers too,' added Allison, a little annoyed George seemed to be taking credit for her discovery.

'Well, thankfully I can dispense with my padding,' and the Ringmaster reached inside his dungarees and pulled out a large fake strap-on stomach. 'I bought this at a theatrical costume shop. Adds to the character, don't you think?'

'It suits you, Mr Jolly,' said George. 'And the 'tache.'

CRACK! The Ringmaster whipped his riding crop down against the pink leather of his boots with a vicious swipe.

'Don't use that name with me, boy. I've left that pathetic old janitor behind. You can address me as Ronald the Ringmaster now!'

George sniggered and Allison giggled too. Even upside down, George couldn't help laughing at his pompousness. Ronald the Ringmaster's face was turning as red as a beetroot.

'Silence!' bellowed the Ringmaster, in a voice as booming as if he were in centre stage, 'I shall have respect.'

The chimpanzees were standing slapping their huge hairy hands together, delighting in their Ringmaster's position of power.

'We're not scared of you, Mr Jolly,' challenged George. 'Once the police find out who you are and what you did, you'll be into jail before you can say 'poo'.'

'Yeah, pink poo!' added Allison, feeling George's courage.

'Oh, but the police don't know and you won't be able tell them. That vat of concentrated poop will be your final resting place only too soon.' Ronald the Ringmaster pointed over to the big tank of churning pink elephant poo and the colour drained from George's face. Allison wasn't sure if his colour drained up or down but he was certainly paler than he was a second ago.

'Those blades will chop your bodies into a million tiny pieces and your blood will merge with the colour of my product.' The Ringmaster snapped his riding crop down on his boots again. 'No one will notice the difference.'

'You will disappear from the face of this earth, just as successfully as I left my previous life....only this time, you two won't be coming back.'

'Swing the pulley, Pippo!' the Ringmaster pointed at the larger ape and then to the arm of the pulley above the swinging net. Pippo hopped across to the lever mechanism and twisted the handle. George and Allison were swung sharply 90degrees towards the tank.

Below them, the vat of pink poo was bubbling and blending as the blades sliced through the fibres and the paddles folded the mixture together again. George's nostrils twitched and he drew in a lungful of air.

'Quite fruity, isn't it?' he suggested. Was he losing his mind?

'We are hanging inches above our impending doom,' growled Allison from behind clenched teeth, 'and you want to discuss the delights of elephant dung?!'

'Mr Ronald, sir?' asked George. 'How did you come up with this delicious aroma, sir?'

'It's a long story, boy. I don't want to bore you to death with it now.'

'But we're going to die in a moment anyway, sir,' argued George gently. 'Those are the rules; the helpless heroes are about to die and the villain always unveils his dastardly plan to conquer the world.'

'I'm not a villain!' the Ringmaster snapped. 'I'm just misunderstood, that's all.'

'I always thought that, sir,' said George softly. 'You were never really suited to being a janitor, were you?'

'No, you're right. I wasn't always a janitor, you know,'

the Ringmaster was staring off into space. 'I studied chemistry and engineering at university. I loved biology. I loved physics. I loved all things science. I actually wanted to be a chemistry teacher.'

'But it was after the third explosion in the science lab, those no-good professors wouldn't let me study there anymore.' Ronald shook his head sadly.

'Keep him talking,' whispered Allison. 'I don't want to end up in that sloppy soup.' But it wasn't difficult to keep the Ringmaster chatting.

'After that, I didn't know what to do with my life. I drifted for a while. I went backpacking around Asia, Australia and the southern continents. That was wonderful.' The sparkle returned to the Ringmaster's eyes. 'I saw many spectacular things. I learned fascinating secrets from lost tribes.'

'Did you know that the aborigines in Australia can breathe in and out at the same time, when they play the didgeridoos? Or that the pygmy tribes in the Bolivian rainforest poison their hunting arrows by rubbing them on the backs of frogs? Or that there are ninja slugs in Malaysia that fire love-darts to attract a mate.' The Ringmaster pulled his shoulders back, proud to show off his knowledge.

'Or did you know that an elephant's faecal deposit contains a powerful hormone called metabolic cortisol, which is only truly understood by the Pu-pu tribe of the African Congo.'

George and Allison twisted inside their net, stared at each other and shook their heads. 'I think he means there's something in their poo,' whispered Allison.

Ronald the Ringmaster sighed. 'No, you wouldn't understand, would you?' he continued. 'I think I am the only person in the land that appreciates this lost science.' He went on...

'Cortisol is an addictive stimulant that also works as a

stress reliever. It promotes feelings of excitement and euphoria. When people drink it, they want more, and it also enhances the flavour of certain related food products.'

'Like burgers?' asked George, trying to sound like he knew what the Ringmaster was talking about.

'Exactly, young man. Like burgers,' agreed the Ringmaster. He pointed his riding crop at George excitedly. 'That's the beauty of this natural chemical. It combines and compliments the fats, bones, cartilage and skeletal tissue found in burgers to make them taste better.'

Allison wrinkled her nose up. 'You don't find bones in burgers?'

'Oh, my dear,' the Ringmaster said with a sad, pitying look on his face. 'How sheltered you are? Bones and cartilage and everything else has always been put in a grinder and turned into burgers.'

'Urgh, barf,' yakked Allison.

'But my secret cortisol chemical makes it all taste beautiful again. And that's why no one will notice you two in the poo stew!' The Ringmaster walked to the end of the platform.

'Wait, Mr Ronald, sir,' cried George, desperate to keep him talking. 'You said, 'when people drink it'. Drink what, exactly?'

The Ringmaster laughed. 'Why, Power Pink, of course!'

'Power Pink?' yelled George, 'The health drink? You mean that you make it here?'

'Certainly, boy. You didn't think this was really just an animal sanctuary, did you?' Ronald the Ringmaster twirled the end of his moustache.

'And the Power Pink drink is actually made from elephant poo?' Allison added.

'Oh yes, we've been collecting pink poo from elephants for months. I learned all about the process when I was in

Africa,' smiled the Ringmaster maliciously, 'and I refined it when I joined the circus, especially by adding beetroot. That was a master stroke.'

'That's why there are beetroot fields all around,' yelled George.

'Yes, what a marvellous vegetable,' grinned the Ringmaster. 'Beetroot contains chemicals that act as muscle relaxants and boosts energy. It increases blood flow and you can exercise for longer after drinking just small quantities of beetroot juice. It's wonderful stuff. Of course, that's where the pink colour comes from.'

The Ringmaster went on, 'And the fruit provides sweetness and fibre and we lace it all with laxatives to keep the elephants, er, flowing regularly, shall we say.'

Allison joined in. 'So, the swimming pool outside isn't really a swimming pool at all?'

'Of course not, stupid girl,' said the Ringmaster impatiently. 'That's the mixing pool, where we take the fresh pink poo from this vat,' he pointed to the large tank beneath them, 'and concentrate it until we achieve the correct consistency, ready for the tankers coming.'

'Then it goes straight to the burger restaurants?' George was feeling sick now, thinking about the poo juice he'd drank in the last couple of days.

'Oh yes! When the boys at McDoballs heard about this magical ingredient, they couldn't wait to get their hands on it,' the Ringmaster laughed. 'It's so highly addictive that sales of their burgers went up by 80% after Power Pink was launched.'

'And because it makes the less-organic matter taste better, McDoballs could add more sawdust into their recipes, thus making the burgers cheaper to produce. Their profits have been rocketing ever since.' Ronald nodded.

'But it's not easy, you know, squeezing those elephants into those tiny cages and now making mincemeat from bags of children. I was a fugitive from the law,' yelled the Ringmaster, a bitterness was creeping back into his voice. 'After that school blew up, I knew I had to escape. Facial surgery doesn't come cheap but I was lucky to test my secret formula on those elephants after I joined the circus.'

There was a loud banging from beyond the barn door and both Pippo and Zippy hopped up and down, slapping the floor with their paws.

'That'll be the delivery tankers back again,' shouted the Ringmaster. 'I'll get the taps open. You two chimps get the doors, the funnels and the hydraulic suction pumps.'

Ronald the Ringmaster waved the two chimps outside. 'We'll deal with these two later.'

Pippo and Zippy swung down from the platform and hopped outside. The Ringmaster wasn't as agile; he stepped down the ramp and walked out through the barn door, leaving George and Allison dangling alone, above the tank of fermenting pink elephant dung.

Chapter 23 - Mental

The institute was a cold, grim building. Set in the bleak wilderness of the northern countryside, three sides of the large, one-storey prison block were surrounded by tall grey walls, whilst a chain link fence, topped off with barbed wire, sealed in the fourth side. A large brass plaque was screwed to the wall at the front and it read:

The Institute for Socially-Challenged Adults in Little Pumpington Mental Establishment

Bars covered every cell window and there was the constant clunk of keys and slamming of doors. Even the windows at the end of each corridor were covered with wire mesh. The obvious purpose of the institute was to remove and incarcerate any unwanted persons from the streets of Little Pumpington, rather than care for, and treat the poor, afflicted individuals.

Hospitalisation was just another word for locking up the town's nutcases so nobody had to feel guilty or embarrassed when they saw them acting strangely.

SCALP-ME was also a rather appropriate name for the country's most backward and narrow-minded mental health hospital. Most patients who entered through heavy iron gates, usually drugged up and drooling, had their heads shaved to cut down on disease and to attach electrodes to their scalps as part of their treatment.

Luckily for Grandpa Jock, who was already bald on top, the medical orderlies who brought him into the night before weren't sure where his hair started and his moustache ended, so they just dressed him in a white cotton hospital gown and chained him to the bed in his cell, with a double set of cuffs.

The task of removing the thick ginger thatch from this disagreeable old Scotsman's head therefore fell upon Big Bertha, the enormous and constantly-agitated state nurse. Bertha's face looked as if it had been slapped with a wet fish everyday throughout her four years of medical training, and she was obviously cultivating the long, thick hairs that grew out of the mole on her chin. She plodded along the corridor, passing cell after cell with a tray balanced expertly on one hand. This contained a mug of shaving foam, an old cut-throat razor, a towel and a syringe full of sedative, just in case the patient objected to the removal of their hair.

In its wisdom, and in its desire to cut costs, the board of SCALP-ME had voted to remove every second fluorescent tube from the lights in the ceiling, leaving the corridors around the mental hospital only half as bright as they were before. The corridor was long, dull, grey and empty, apart from a heavy ceramic water fountain at the end.

Bertha waddled slowly until she reached the appropriate cell but she was surprised to see that the door was already slightly open. This was against hospital policy, she raged silently; cells should always be kept locked. And when she pushed the door fully open she was horrified to witness another serious breach of security; the bed, upon which the inmate should have been strapped to, was empty. There was one set of chains and cuffs, meant to restrain the patient, lying in a heap on the pillow. The other set was missing.

Bertha laid the tray on the bed and examined the locks. These were high-tensile steel handcuffs designed to stop even the maddest of mental patients from cutting, breaking or chewing their way through them. Yet these locks looked as if they'd been popped open, with a key! But the only keys were kept locked in the nurses' station and had all been accounted for, both at evening and morning inspection.

Then Bertha noticed something on the floor. She bent down onto her chubby hands and fat knees to take a closer look at the little pink pile on the tiles. She picked one up and stared at it. It was a thick, stained fingernail.

The other nails in the pile had once belonged to various fingers, thumbs and toes, all tainted pink and all recently chewed off. She turned and examined the door. Again, there was no damage yet it had been opened from the inside; there was still a thick fingernail sticking out of the slot. The lock had been picked.

CRASH!!!

There was a shattering of breaking glass and grinding of sheet metal fencing coming from the end of the corridor. Bertha lurched onto her knees and dragged herself to her feet using the end of the bed. She wobbled into the corridor and felt the hairs on her mole tickle as the wind blew through the smashed window.

She walked to the opening and looked down. A few feet below, in the courtyard, was the water fountain lying amongst a heap of broken glass and window debris.

Bertha looked up. Scraps of white material were torn on the barbed wire.

Way, way off in the distance she could just make out a shock of ginger hair, below which was part of a shredded hospital gown flapping wildly in the wind and the little white bum of an elderly ex-inmate running off into the trees.

Chapter 24 – Hanging Around

'What just happened here?' Allison was usually very sharp but the last few minutes had been such a blur she was still trying to catch up. Her world had been turned upside-down in more ways than one.

'Well, we're hanging above a large vat of fragrant elephant poo, awaiting our doom at the hands of a deranged ex-janitor,' explained George, feeling the blood rushing to his head.

'Yes, I know that,' snapped Allison, 'but what about this pink stuff? Surely he was only kidding about drinking it?'

'I don't think so,' said George. 'This is quite a production line they've got going here. I saw those chimpanzees collecting the pink poo at the parade so they've just graduated to something bigger.'

'I suppose there is a demand for that drink at McDoballs,' Allison said with a shrug (or as much of a shrug as she could manage hanging upside-down in a net). 'And look at how addicted Kenny was to the stuff.'

'But let me get this straight,' Allison went on, 'Ronald the Ringmaster discovered the power of elephant poo when he was back-packing round the world as a failed student, right?'

'Right…' agreed George, 'and he was able to experiment on those elephants when he ran away with the circus….'

'….after our school exploded.' Allison finished his sentence. 'He said he'd blown up three laboratories at university. I suppose he knew how to look after himself in a blast.'

'Yes! That's how he survived!' yelled George, the net pressing into his cheek.

'But what does this Power Pink juice actually do?' asked Allison. 'We know it's very addictive.'

'The poster in McDoballs said it came from Nature's larder,' said George. 'That it's an all-natural, fruit-based health drink.'

'I think we know it's a little too close to nature now.' Allison couldn't believe she'd drank the stuff. 'And what did Ronald call it? A metabolic cortisol?'

'Yeah,' replied George, 'the metabolic bit must mean that it burns off calories. That's why they said it helped people lose weight.'

'Not judging by all those fat people in the restaurant, it doesn't' said Allison.

'That's because they were addicted to eating more and more burgers.' George could see now that a product that made people excited, happy and relaxed was something that customers would crave. 'And it made food taste better, even the less organic parts like bone and cartilage and sawdust.'

'Your Grandpa thought they put poo in burgers,' said Allison, 'I wasn't expecting them to make us drink poo juice too.'

'Oh but I do!' said the Ringmaster, entering the barn again. He'd been listening to their conversation from the edge of the tank.

'That's another ten tankers filled with Power Pink concentrate being delivered to fast food restaurants all over the country.' The Ringmaster was exuberant. 'Today, Britain. Tomorrow, the world.'

'Sadly, children, you won't be around to witness my Power Pink world domination. Pippo, unlock the crank. Lower away!'

The two chimpanzees had walked in behind the Ringmaster with their knuckles clumping on the floor. Pippo leapt up onto the top platform and hopped across to the red crank handle. Zippy stayed down on the floor next to the Ringmaster.

Pippo held onto the handle and slipped the brake off. The wheel began to turn slowly anti-clockwise. George and Allison descended into the pink, sloppy dung puddle.

The blades went on whirring around the vat, cutting through the mush with razor-sharp ease. The paddles churned the mixture over. George's nose twitched as the fruity perfume aroma rose from the dung.

'It could be worse,' said George. 'This stuff could stink.'

'I'm not worried about the smell at this moment, George,' said Allison, her eyes spinning as she watched the blades rotate.

Closer and closer they dropped, lower and lower. Their heads were inches above the bubbling surface of the poo. It plopped and splattered as the paddles turned it over. As soon as they hit the liquid they'd be dragged under and sliced through by the blades. At least it would be quick.

'I suppose this is it then,' sighed George. He tried to wriggle free but the net was holding him tight and he could hardly wiggle his toes.

'What a way to go...' squealed Allison, her voice cracking with tension '...drowned in dung.'

'We'll be chopped up before we can drown, Allison!'

Pippo was still holding the handle, edging George and Allison closer to their fate.

'That's it, Pippo, slowly.' The Ringmaster seemed to be enjoying their demise. 'I don't want you to drop them and splash any of our precious liquid now.'

Pippo stopped turning the handle. There was a low trundling sound, barely audible above the noise of the pump engine. The chimp looked around. Flying towards him at break-neck pace was some kind of madman wearing a torn hospital gown... on a scooter! The wheels rumbled on the wooden floor otherwise the surprise attack would've been completely silent.

Ginger hair was blowing around wildly and the hospital gown was flapping in the breeze. Just before impact Grandpa Jock raised his right hand. In it, he was holding handcuffs on a chain.

The scooter crashed into the startled chimpanzee, throwing him backwards. The chimp flew through the air, off the end of the walkway and splashed down into the doo-doo tank. At the same moment, the chain of the handcuffs smashed down and wrapped around the crank handle, jamming the release mechanism. The rope stuck tight. Grandpa Jock hit the big red emergency cut-off switch and the blades stopped turning.

George and Allison's eyes flicked to the side as they'd just watched the hairy chimp fly past them and splat into the watery pink dung. By cutting the electricity to the blades the chimp had avoided becoming a chopped-up mess so instead, Pippo splashed above the surface before being dragged down into the tank and sucked along the large pipe into the laboratory. The power to the blades was off but the suction pump was still working.

'That was unexpected,' said George calmly.

'That could've been us!' yelled Allison, shocked to hear George sounding so cool.

'Hang on, you two,' shouted the familiar voice, 'we'll soon have you doon!'

'About time too, Grandpa!' shrieked George, finally realising how close they'd come.

'Swing the pulley over that way, lad,' shouted Grandpa Jock, giving the thumbs-up to Crayon Kenny on the other side of the platform. George and Allison twisted in their net to catch a glimpse of their friend as he yanked the lever mechanism back the way it had come and the pulley swung away from the poo tank.

'Get them!' yelled Ronald the Ringmaster to Zippy but the

startled chimp was still too shocked by the disappearance of his big brother. One moment he'd been there, the next he was gone.

The Ringmaster wasn't hanging around. He wasn't about to let his poop juice dream be wrecked by three meddling kids and a half-naked, mad old man. He ran up the ramp towards the upper level.

But Kenny ran faster. He sprinted over to the elephant cages and began sliding the bolts across and throwing open the cage doors. Fruit and beetroot scattered across the floor as the elephants pressed their way out of their prisons. Luckily, in blowing off their last bit of bottom build-up the elephants were just thin enough again to squeeze out of the cages.

It was Nelly the elephant, who'd been carefully watching, who took the lead. She was one of the first elephants to be freed and blasted a full trunk trumpet into the air and charged towards the top of the ramp....

To be met by Ronald the Ringmaster running up the ramp towards her. They both skidded, stopped and stared at each other, like two gunslingers, ready for a shoot out.

It was at that precise moment that the Ringmaster realised that if this really was a shoot-out then Nelly the elephant was metaphorically packing a far bigger gun. Ronald had his whip in his hand but Nelly was six tons of angry charging elephant, aimed downhill, locked and loaded.

The Ringmaster saw in Nelly's eyes every single one of the beatings, the rants and the humiliation that he'd put those elephants through in the last twelve months. Elephants never forget.

Wisely, Ronald the Ringmaster turned and ran. He ran down the ramp faster than he'd ever run in his life. A raging elephant behind you does have that effect.

The Ringmaster sprinted passed the bewildered Zippy at the bottom and into the laboratory.

This snapped Zippy out of his state of shock just in time for the chimp to leap up onto the vat of poo and hold on to the side of the tank as Nelly and the herd of charging elephants crashed through the barn door below him.

Kenny had done his job well, releasing all the elephants and the stampede kept coming. Grandpa Jock had carefully removed the handcuffs from the crank handle and was lowering George and Allison down onto the ground on the other side of the poop tank.

The huge barn door was smashed to pieces by the force of the elephants. Daylight shone into the barn now and George was blinking again as he untangled himself from the net. Allison pointed outside and in the courtyard was the most extraordinary sight.

Standing there was the TV director, with his back to the edge of the laboratory and a camera on his shoulder. He turned to give a big thumbs-up to Grandpa Jock, who was walking down the ramp towards them.

'I tripped him up, Jock' shouted the TV director, 'Just like you said.'

'That's Tarquin the TV director,' panted Grandpa Jock.

'Nice scooter skills, Mr Jock,' said Allison.

'Yeah, great rescue, Grandpa,' agreed George, 'but where's my scooter?'

'Oh, I left it up there,' said Grandpa Jock, pointing back up to the cage platform. 'I thought the ramp looked too steep. But I see somebody is on the slippery slope.'

*

McDOBALLS

From: *Operations Director Ronald*
To: *Chief Operating Officer*
Cc: *Marketing Director*
Subject: Security Breach!!

Sir,

I regret to inform you that there has been a serious 'incident' at the production centre. The juice producers have escaped. Recommend full damage limitation and shut down of production facilities until normal service can be resumed.

Regards

Ronald

PS There's a large, angry ape in the lab. It's going to throw me out of the win.............

Chapter 26 – Time To Set Your Watch

The large, angry ape, well technically a chimpanzee, did throw Ronald the Ringmaster through the window.

And outside Tarquin the TV director was focussing his camera at the crowd of twenty elephants gathered in the middle of the courtyard. The jumbos had formed a loose circle and in the middle was Ronald, looking very frightened. His brash confidence was gone, his eyes wide and searching for an escape route.

Every time he made a bolt for a gap in the circle, one of the elephants would nudge him back into the centre with their head. He was trapped and going nowhere.

George, Allison, Kenny and Grandpa Jock ran from the shed to join Tarquin outside. He was grinning wildly.

'This is brilliant, darlings,' he kept saying, 'I'll win an Oscar for this.'

At first, there was just a slight rumble; a gurgling, bubbling noise.

Then, a little squeak.

Followed by a parp and a pump.

In the centre of the ring of elephants the Ringmaster looked at his watch. He'd always said that he had his head so far up the elephants' bottoms that he could set the clock by their bowel movements. That time had come.

Together, the elephants made a beautiful turning motion in unison, all moving at the same time, in the same direction, like a chorus line of jumbo ballerinas. As they pirouetted around, George was sure he saw the elephants smiling again.

They were now facing outwards, bottoms pressed together in a tight circle. Ronald the Ringmaster was caught in the middle, with twenty elephants' bums pointing right towards him.

A short poop, then a long trumpet blast. Then another. A series of bowel shuddering quakes rumbled onwards. The laxatives were working and once again the air was filled with that warm ripe aroma as every elephant began to unblock their logs. Looks of relief spread across each animal's face as they sighed collectively.

With a few final squeaks, the dumping was done. The empty elephants began to drift apart. In the middle of the circle remained a pile of pink poo over two metres tall. The plugged-up pachyderms had once again blasted their bottoms, this time dropping a dump truck full of dung onto the unfortunate Ringmaster. Only a pair of pink boots poked out from beneath the poop.

'Do you think he suffocated?' asked Allison.

'I think the sheer force of the blast might have knocked him out,' Grandpa Jock suggested. 'At least I hope it did. He's not going to want to remember much about this.'

George was counting on his fingers and running numbers in his head. 'An elephant can dump up to 100kg of poop each time, right? And I reckon there were about twenty elephants surrounding him.'

'What's your point, George?' asked Allison, not really sure if she wanted to know the answer.

'That means Ronald over there is lying under nearly two tons of poop,' announced George, pleased with his math skills.

'I know I should be disgusted but I suppose he deserved it,' said Allison smiling.

Kenny was staring at the enormous pile of poo.

'Why is the poo pink?' he asked.

George and Allison just looked at each other. Up until that moment they were the only ones who knew about the Power Pink secret.

George winked. 'Shall you tell him or can I?' George was going to enjoy this.

Just then, one of the other laboratory windows smashed and a pink chimpanzee, whose hair was thickly matted with elephant dung, leapt through.

Chapter 27 – Butt Monkey

Five minutes earlier Pippo had thrown Ronald the Ringmaster out of the window in a fit of anger and revenge. He had not been expecting to be hit by a maniac on a scooter, dumped in the juice tank, or to be flushed along a pipe into the laboratory, so when he saw the Ringmaster crouched over the computer, he couldn't stop himself from grabbing Ronald by the collar and launching him through the window.

Then he paused to munch a couple of bananas that were lying in the feeding tray. If he'd known there was a herd of angry elephants waiting outside he'd have stayed in the lab but he hopped through the broken window and nearly passed out with fright. He was surrounded by jumbos and his little brother Zippy was perched on top of the sludge tank screeching loudly.

Pippo's world stopped!

They weren't bad chimps, thought Pippo, they'd just had a rough ride. What had they done to deserve all this? Born in captivity, in an animal testing centre, they were forced to smoke 100 cigarettes a day. Zippy still had a nasty cough. Make-up and lipstick was rubbed into their eyes to check if it was safe for humans.

But they'd escaped and they joined a circus. Pippo and Zippy made themselves indispensable, mucking out the cages, cleaning equipment and helping to put up the Big Top until the Ringmaster promoted them to Chimps-in-Charge. It was a rather sudden change and they weren't cut out for leadership but the Ringmaster insisted. Cattle prods and bull-whips seemed to be the best way to motivate the other animals.

And the elephants were now ready to remind the chimps about their 'positive reinforcement'.

Now it was time to make a quick getaway. Pippo grabbed at a trunk and swung upwards, yanking on the elephant's nose. He hopped onto a tusk, bounded across a couple of heads and swung down to the ground on a big flappy ear. It was much easier to swing when you're not wearing size 35 clown shoes.

Zippy was still perched on the tank screeching wildly and pointing out into the courtyard but just as Pippo reached the vat he heard a bellowing trumpet behind him. He turned to see six tons of grey muscle charging towards him. It was Smelly.

Pippo jumped up onto the platform, just as the elephant crashed into the wooden vat. Zippy saw this coming too and joined his brother.

Smelly's tusks pierced the side of the tank and she was stuck fast. Pink poo juice was seeping from the giant barrel. The wood was splitting and bursting, pouring more and more beetroot bum liquid all over the barn and the courtyard as Smelly tried to pull free. The other elephants were sliding about as the sloppy skitter mixture flooded out over the floor.

High above Pippo and Zippy had spied George's scooter, abandoned by Grandpa Jock, and the cheeky chimps were now using it to make a quick getaway, hurtling down the ramp at 40 miles an hour.

'This is not going to be good,' said Grandpa Jock.

Smelly was still jerking her head furiously backwards, trying to loosen her tusks from the wood.

The chimps were going faster.

Smelly pulled herself free with an almighty tug. She stumbled backwards.

The scooter hit the bottom of the ramp too fast.

'Don't look, Allison,' said George, trying to cover her eyes. Allison pushed aside George's attempts to protect her.

The front wheel of the scooter twisted into the ground and stopped dead in its tracks. Unfortunately, Pippo and Zippy didn't stop. Momentum carried the hairy chimps up and over the handlebars. They flew through air, still travelling at over 40 miles an hour.

Smelly stumbled backwards.

The chimps flew forwards.

They all met in the middle.

SCHPLOTCH!!!

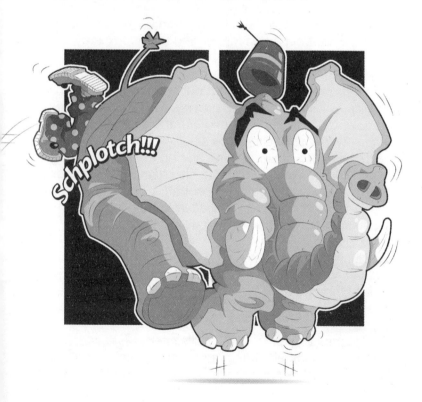

'Ooooooooooh,' winced George, Kenny, Allison and Grandpa Jock, all at the same time. Tarquin was too busy capturing the moment on his camera to feel the pain.

Pippo and Zippy had both flown head first, straight up the elephant's butt. Of course moments before, Smelly had just deposited her fruity bowel contents over the unfortunate Ringmaster and with all that fibre and laxative in her diet, her poop was loose and watery. Her butt was wet and greasy.

Pippo and Zippy had plunged deep into the elephant's bum, right up to their knees and now only four little chimp feet were sticking out her bottom.

Smelly wasn't happy either. The startled elephant blew off a loud trumpet blast and ran around the courtyard with the hairy little chimp legs poking out of her rear end.

Finally, the vat of poo gave up trying to hold itself together and burst open wide, spilling thousands of gallons of pink watery poo juice all over the ground. A giant tidal wave of turd flowed out of the barn and into the courtyard.

Kenny was first to slip in the sludgy tsunami. He went down on his bottom and rolled around in the poo, trying to get up. George was next, losing his balance as the river of slop flowed over his feet. He grabbed at his Grandpa Jock for balance and he was pulled down too. Allison slipped. Tarquin slipped and his camera was lost beneath a wave of pink poop.

Gradually the wave subsided as the contents of the poo tank spread out thinly across the ground. George and his Grandpa Jock clambered to their feet. They helped up Tarquin, then Allison and finally, a very wet, pink Crayon Kenny.

The scene before them was a disaster.

There were pink elephants rolling around in their own poo juice. Smelly the elephant was still upset, running around with two monkeys stuck up her butt and there was a pair of pink wellington boots sticking out from underneath two tons of elephant plop.

Beeep, beep, beeeeeeeep.

'That's my phone,' said Tarquin, fumbling around with his dripping wet crimson camera. He plucked the mobile from the holster clipped onto his belt and read the text message.

'I'll call the police and the fire brigade to clear up this mess,' said the TV director, looking across at Smelly still charging across the courtyard. 'And maybe a vet too.'

He continued, 'We've got a press conference to go to!'

Chapter 28 – The Press Conference

In the TV van heading towards the press conference, Grandpa Jock explained to George and Allison how he'd visualised the danger they were in, whilst he was recovering in the mad house. The pink poo, McDoballs and the addictive drink George had told him about; it all fitted together.

Grandpa Jock knew they were in danger so he escaped from the mental hospital using his old army skills and a few toe-nail clippings and ran round to Kenny's house to drag him out of his sick bed. Then Grandpa Jock called the TV director who'd filmed the fake elephant party and offered him the chance to record an exclusive Pulitzer Prize winning exposé. Of course, Tarquin jumped at the chance.

'And I've captured it all on film, darlings,' added the director. 'The confession, the death threats, the caged elephants, everything.'

'But where are we going now?' asked George, his head a swirl with new information.

'McDoballs have called an emergency press conference this afternoon,' announced Tarquin, driving like a maniac.

George nodded quietly, realising his opportunity. During the rest of the journey he took time to explain his whole theory to everyone.

*

The press conference was being held in a large hotel in the City Centre, a few miles away from Little Pumpington. Tarquin had flashed his press pass at the security guard and abandoned his van in the basement car park. The five of them ran up the back stairs and into the convention hall just as the press conference was getting under way and everyone stopped and turned as five, pink poo-covered intruders burst through the doors at the back of the room. Tarquin straightened himself up, brushed off pieces of imaginary poop from his jacket and coughed,

'Ahem,' he said, 'carry on, darlings.' He was trying to look as professional as it's possible to look covered in elephant poop.

The McDoballs Head of Marketing, Mr B.S.Woffel, had been ordered by the Chief Operating Officer to make a rare public appearance, in order to manipulate any news about the elephant sanctuary incident before it… ahem… leaked out, so to speak. He was standing on a small stage at the front, with a McDoballs logo behind him. He wore a sharp suit, with an even sharper beard and looked impressively confident.

George whispered, 'I don't trust him.' George didn't trust anyone with a beard. Men with beards usually had 'issues'. What did they have to hide? Men with beards always seemed rather shifty. Were they just too lazy to shave? And if they were too lazy to shave, were they too lazy to wash properly? Men with beards seemed to have personal hygiene issues, usually involving bits of food stuck in there for days.

Blackbeard the Pirate definitely had anger issues. 'Bluto' from the Popeye cartoons had a beard and he was another nasty piece of work. Vikings were always fighting and pillaging, and women with beards were almost as bad. George didn't trust anyone with a beard unless their name was Santa.

B.S Woffel smiled a fake smile from behind his beard and he carried on talking

'The unprecedented success of our unique health drink Power Pink has meant that demand has far exceeded supply. We're simply unable to cope with the volumes required.'

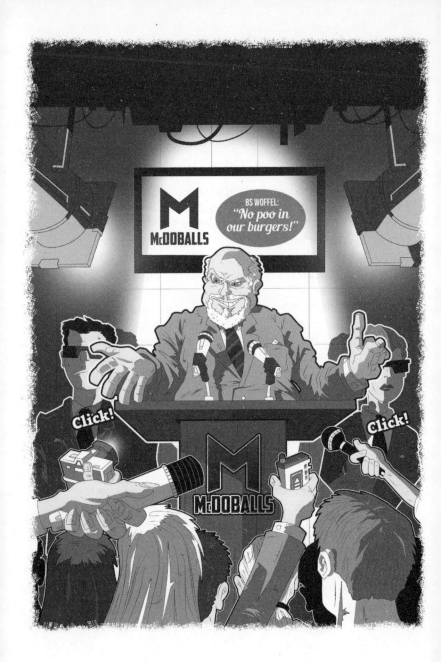

'That is why we are removing Power Pink from sale in McDoballs with immediate effect.'

There was a groan from the audience. A number of large men and women there were already addicted to the product themselves.

'Will Power Pink ever be going back on sale?' shouted a voice from the press pack.

'At this stage, we're not sure,' the Marketing Executive grinned. 'Perhaps once we've been able to secure sufficient stock, then it's possible but I couldn't put any timescales on that.'

Tarquin was messing about with his camera and George nudged him in the ribs. The TV director looked anxiously at George and stood up.

'Are you able to tell us Power Pink's secret ingredient?' Tarquin was greeted by sniggers from the audience and another false grin from the Head of Marketing.

'Of course, the recipe for Power Pink is a closely guarded secret,' he schmoozed. 'I couldn't possibly divulge such a valuable piece of information.'

Tarquin was about to sit down again, perhaps too easily, when George and Allison poked at him again. The TV director didn't look convinced.

'But it won't....' gasped Tarquin.

'Get up and tell them, Tarky,' urged George, with Allison helping to push him forward again.

'Er, one more question, sir,' asked Tarquin. 'Would Power Pink's secret ingredient happen to be elephant poo?' he asked quickly, and sat back down again.

The colour drained from Woffel's face. He tried to grin again. It came out more like a grimace. 'That would be...er... ridiculous, wouldn't it?' he paused, not quite sure what to say next. George jumped up,

'You make that pink stuff out of elephant poo and you're

127

poisoning the country with it!' he yelled.

'Y-you'd better have some proof to back up that statement, young man,' stammered the Head of Marketing, almost ready to faint. But the press men weren't looking at him, they'd all turned towards George.

'We've got all the proof we need right here,' announced George, turning to Tarquin.

'I tried to tell you,' the TV director hissed.

'Tell us what?' asked Allison.

'It's all this muck in the camera,' he shrugged. 'I've lost all the film.'

'What? All of it?' whispered George.

'Yes, I think so,' said Tarquin and there was a silent pause across the audience. Without being able to hear what they were whispering about from the front, the McDoballs Marketing man sensed this delay as a sign of weakness in their case. He recovered himself and went on the attack.

'McDoballs take such ludicrous allegations very seriously,' he fired off. 'You will be facing our army of highly paid lawyers and we will drag you through the courts and down into the gutter to fight such damaging accusations.'

George stared at poor Tarquin again and the TV director looked back apologetically, 'The disk is corrupted with jobby juice. I can't do anything. I'm sorry.'

The McDoballs man was on a roll now. 'Unless you have categorical proof to back up your preposterous claims, then I suggest you retract your statement regarding our product.'

Woffel went on, 'I can confirm, here and now, that McDoballs burgers are quality products made from the finest British beef, with no artificial additives.'

George looked crest-fallen. He couldn't prove anything. But it was Grandpa Jock's turn to leap to his feet, still covered in pink poo.

'But we know McDoballs are in partnership with Eazy-

PeeZee charity up at the elephant sanctuary, aren't they?' demanded Grandpa Jock.

'And isn't it the Eazy-PeeZee Cheese company that produces the melted cheese for all McDoballs restaurants?' George and Allison's eyes widened as Grandpa Jock went on ranting.

'No comment!'

'What about Eazy-PeeZee Treeze Ltd? The timber company in Scotland? McDoballs add their sawdust into the burgers, don't you?' Grandpa Jock was going for the jugular.

'You don't expect to be taken seriously, looking like that!'

Grandpa Jock continued, ignoring the fact that he was covered in pink, elephant poo.

'And Eazy PeeZee Squeezy Ltd? They're an invisible holding company for the firm that make the laxative Fibre-Flush!' There was silence throughout the hall. Grandpa Jock finished up triumphantly, 'And you're feeding those laxatives to the elephants.'

The assembled press pack was staring at Grandpa Jock with wide-mouthed amazement; it was a fantastic story. First, there was a snigger, then a giggle and a guffaw before the entire audience burst out laughing. They were almost wetting themselves; some of the journalists were holding their sides, others were slapping their thighs. Their faces were beetroot red with laughter.

'That's brilliant,' one reporter wheezed. 'Very funny!'

'That's unbelievable,' another gasped.

'Even we couldn't make that up,' said a third, panting heavily.

Woffel seized his opportunity. 'Ladies and gentlemen of the media, occasionally some poor deluded fool will read one of the many conspiracy theories on the internet and believe it to be the truth. Some years ago a cola company was accused of passing off tap water as mineral water; pure fabrication, of coures. But these claims...' He threw back his hand in a dismissive fashion, '...are complete fantasy!'

'Let me assure you,' he went on, 'there is no poo in our burgers, elephant or otherwise. And you can quote me on that! Thank you and goodbye.'

The Marketing Executive marched off the stage quickly and vanished through a side door. A large security guard, with an explosion of nostril hair protruding, stepped in front of the door; no one else was leaving that way. The press conference was officially over.

The journalists and reporters packed up their bags, their cameras and their microphones. As they walked passed, they'd smile and nod 'Nice one,' or 'Really funny.'

'But it's true,' George was still protesting. 'It's all true.' But none of the press pack took any more notice; to them, it was just some young attention seeker looking for the limelight.

'Come on, lad,' Grandpa Jock said, putting his hand on George's shoulder. 'Some people just can't handle the truth.'

McDOBALLS

The McDoballs Corporation

From: *Chief Operating Officer*
To: *All Department Executives*
Subject: Operation Addictive Elephant Project X Update

Ladies and gentlemen,

I have just arrived back from Ground Zero by corporate helicopter and our sanctuary project is a mess. I have ordered the facilities be shut down immediately and the press have been paid off. It has cost McDoballs a lot of money but absolutely necessary.

The TV director has been warned that if he breathes a word of this to anyone, he'll be blacklisted and never work in television again.

Below are your tasks in the rest of this damage limitation process.

Marketing: *Pull Power Pink from the menu. Run 'Go Large' campaign on all other soft drinks. Release a follow-up statement, hinting that tiny amounts of bone and cartilage may have entered the rending process as a faulty part of production but that has now been rectified.*

Production: *To ensure any tests that are carried out do NOT detect any bone and sawdust matter, we should remove the wood pulp, sawdust and all other artificial additives from our burgers for a short time.*

Finance: *Whilst I appreciate that you will object to pure beef being too expensive, this will be safer in the long run. Be prepared to bribe, blackmail and 'persuade' any testing parties on the purity of our products, as usual.*

Operations: *We will be requiring a new Head of Operations. Ronald the Ringmaster is now indisposed. In response to environmental pressures, I recommend a change in the colour of our restaurants. Currently they are pink and yellow; however, it may be wiser to disassociate ourselves from the colour pink at the moment. I recommend we change to more 'earthy' colours, like green and brown, creating little environmentally friendly havens of rainforest in our restaurants.*

Finance: *Please source some really cheap green and brown paint that is not too toxic.'*

Finally, the McDoballs Corporation still technically owns the elephants. I recommend that when their poo returns to its normal colour, we use the dung to make paper cups and bio-degradable bags, as this would be cheaper for the raw materials.
   Customers will be quick to accept this. They are lazy, fat and stupid and they will keep eating anything we want to feed them.

Yours sincerely
C.O.O.

Chapter 30 – A Few Days Later

George and Allison were pushing their bikes towards the little newsagent's shop just around the corner from their homes. They'd had an eventful few days and were happy to be taking things easy now.

'I'm glad those vets were able to remove those chimps from that elephant's butt,' said George in a matter-of-fact fashion.

'They said it was a tricky job though,' replied Allison. 'A six hour operation, apparently. Both chimps were wedged right up there.'

'Still, both Pippo and Zippy seem to be quite happy mucking out up at the elephant sanctuary. Happy to help, it seems, now they're not in charge any more.'

Allison chuckled, 'And Nelly and her elephants will make sure they don't misbehave again.'

'Just shows what can happen if you're led astray by the wrong company,' replied George.

'And how long did it take to dig out Mr Jolly, or should I say Ronald the Ringmaster, again? Three hours, wasn't it?'

'Yeah,' laughed George, 'Three hours buried in a steaming pile of elephant poop. He's definitely not jolly now. Prison will be a pleasure after all that.

'It was nice of all those supermarkets to offer to send their out of date fruit and vegetables to the elephants, instead of dumping it. That'll keep the jumbos well fed.'

'And proper animal charities will help out too,' said George. 'They'll be well looked after now.'

As they walked up to the front of the newsagents, they saw a row of billboards, advertising the news headlines. George grunted and pointed at the Little Pumpington Bugle. It read...

McDOBALLS BURGERS DO NOT CONTAIN POO!

'That's hardly news, is it?' said George. 'Burgers do not contain poo? I would have thought that was a basic requirement.'

'I suppose some people will believe whatever big companies tell them,' replied Allison.

'But I can't believe they're getting away with it,' argued George. 'My grandpa was right. Large corporations are a bunch of pirates.'

'Where is your grandpa anyway?' asked Allison. 'I haven't seen him around for a couple of days.'

'The mad old tube wants to get himself into the Guinness Book of Records,' said George shaking his head. 'By becoming the oldest man to scooter around the British Isles in a kilt!'

'On a motorised scooter, surely?' giggled Allison.

'No, on my kick scooter,' replied George, 'He's said he was going out to practise on it right now.'

'He's daft as a brush, your Grandpa. I hope I'm that adventurous when I'm that age.'

'What age?' replied George. 'He doesn't know how old he is.'

'Exactly!' said Allison, 'It doesn't matter how old you are to have fun.'

'Talking of daft as brushes, here comes Kenny,' said George, pointing down the road. Kenny was racing up the hill, pedalling furiously. His face was red and he was panting hard. His bike skidded to a halt in front of George and Allison but he was too out of breath to talk.

'I'm glad he's chosen to give up burgers now,' remarked George, turning to Allison. 'It might help his fitness a bit.'

'I'm not surprised he's quitting fast food, after he saw the juice ingredients first hand,' smiled Allison. Kenny just stuck his tongue out, as if gagging.

'George,' he gasped, 'George, you've got to come quick.

134

It's your grandpa. He's on the roof of McDoballs!'

'No! You're joking!' shrieked George. 'They'll lock him up again for sure.'

'He's dyed his hair pink and he's protesting on their roof.' shouted Kenny, finally getting his breath back.

'Come on, George. Let's go,' yelled Allison and jumped on her bike. George was stunned but it didn't take him long to recover and was soon catching up with Allison and Kenny. They reached the restaurant in record time.

A large crowd had formed outside the burger bar to watch the pink-haired pensioner march up and down on the roof of the burger bar. Grandpa Jock had dyed his ginger hair a shocking magenta colour. From a distance George thought he was wearing a pink toga but as he came closer, George realised that Grandpa Jock had two large pieces of material wrapped round his body.

'George, hey George,' he shouted from the roof and waving his arms wildly, 'How d'ya like my pink poo protest? I couldn't get a pink kilt so I washed my white bed sheets with my red socks. What d'ya think? Brilliant, eh!'

At the front of the crowd there were the same two policemen who'd arrested Grandpa Jock the first time.

They were there for crowd safety but most of the audience were enjoying Grandpa Jock's performance. One of policemen was carrying a loud speaker.

'**SIR, YOU ARE CAUSING AN ILLEGAL OBSTRUCTION, SIR,**' blared the sergeant.

Grandpa Jock started singing, 'Shove your megaphone up your bum! Shove, your mega-phone, up your bum!'

'**SIR, YOU ARE COMMITTING A PUBLIC ORDER OFFENCE. IF YOU DO NOT COME DOWN IMMEDIATELY, YOU WILL BE ARRESTED!**' blasted the policeman, and the crowd began to boo him loudly.

'Shove your mega-phone, shove your mega-phone....'

Grandpa Jock went on.

'Power to the Pink Pensioner!' yelled one man at the front.

'Pink to make the girls wink!' screamed a group of old ladies in their seventies, waving their handbags over their heads and wolf-whistling up. One of the old dears whistled too hard and spat out her false teeth. Luckily she caught them in her handbag.

'PLEASE DO NOT ENCOURAGE HIM, LADIES AND GENTLEMEN!' called the policeman to the crowd, **'IT WILL ONLY MAKE HIM WORSE!'**

And it did. Grandpa Jock grinned madly. He was winning the crowd over and thrilled about it. He started dancing a crazy jig, kicking his legs up and waving the large banner that was stuck onto the handlebars of George's folding scooter. It read...

Don't Eat McDoballs Bum Burgers – Made From Real Poo!

And the crowd was getting busier. Grandpa Jock's wild antics were drawing more and more people to come and watch. People were holding up their phones and filming the crazy pink dancer on the roof. George looked at all the little mobiles and iPads that people were playing with. He peered over shoulders to see what they were doing, and Grandpa Jock was on the screen!

'Look. He's on YouTube,' George nudged Allison. 'Somebody has uploaded my grandpa onto the internet.' Allison stared over at the little dancing pink man on the page.

'And they think he's a mentalist too,' said Allison, pointing at the caption. PINK DANCING CLOWN another video title read. And another video was posted. And another. The first caption had now received over one million hits in little over twenty minutes and was being shared across the world.

'Grandpa, you're going viral,' yelled George.

'No, I'm not' Grandpa Jock shouted back, 'I feel fine.'

The street was now jammed packed with on-lookers. Cars were blocking the road and honking their horns. Drivers wound down their car windows to get a better look at the mad man on the roof.

'Hey, it's that guy from the radio!' shouted one of the drivers, pointing up to Grandpa Jock.

Allison put her head in her hands. 'Oh no,' she said, 'He's been on the radio news now. He's a laughing stock.'

'And here comes the television cameras too,' added Kenny as the TV news van double-parked on the main road and the crew jumped out and started filming. George recognised Tarquin and squeezed his way through the crowd. He pulled at the TV director's sleeve.

'Hey, my grandpa's protest was meant to be serious,' accused George. 'And you've turned it into a circus. You've seen the truth – why are you still filming this?'

'I've got to make a living somehow, darling,' said Tarquin, turning back to his cameraman. 'That's it. Focus in on his pink hair and the bald patch.' George returned to the front.

'COME DOWN NOW, OR YOU WILL BE ARRESTED'

Grandpa Jock lifted up his pink bed sheets and waved his bottom at the crowd. The audience went wild with appreciation.

'Alright constable, arrest that man.' The sergeant put down his loud hailer, ordering the constable to enter the building.

'You can't arrest him,' yelled George. 'He has a legitimate protest. He's trying to help.'

'The boy's right,' said a voice from the doorway. It was a spotty young man in a pink and yellow McDoballs shirt with a paper hat on his head. His name badge read 'Brian – Manager' and judging by the number of gold stars he had decorating the strap around his neck, he'd worked there for a long time.

'The boy's right,' Brian the manager said again. 'You can't arrest that man.'

George, Allison and Kenny all blinked at the most unlikely ally. Why was the McDoballs manager coming to Grandpa Jock's help?

'This has been our busiest day for months,' Brian said. 'The Prancing Pink Pensioner has attracted more customers today than any advertising campaign could ever do. He's brilliant. Can he stay?'

So Grandpa Jock's plan had backfired. Eventually when he came down from the roof, he had to stay hidden in the freezer of McDoballs restaurant until the crowd had dispersed. It took nearly two hours to return the street to normal and the police gave him a real ticking off.

McDoballs Head Office had seen Grandpa Jock on the news too and they'd called the manager to tell him they did not want to press charges. It was good for business at the time but they felt it was now best to sweep the whole matter under the carpet, in case anybody looked too closely.

Grandpa Jock had hoped to raise awareness about the quality of the burgers, those extra little ingredients and the exploitation of people who were simply addicted to fast food. Instead, he'd help sell more burgers in one day than most restaurants sell in a week.

'Look on the bright side, Grandpa,' laughed George, trying to make him feel better, 'At least you're famous, as the Prancing Pink Pensioner.'

'Mr Jock,' added Allison, 'people will only believe what they want. One man can't change everybody's mind.'

'And I guess the odd burger now and again wouldn't do me any harm,' shrugged Kenny. George stared over at his burger loving buddy. It was a losing battle. Even after everything Kenny had seen and smelled and swam in, he still wanted to eat fast food.

'Next time,' said Grandpa Jock, 'I'm going to bring a bigger sign.'

'And next time, I'm going to bring the elephants,' winked George.

'You're right lad,' Grandpa Jock added. 'Any protest about pink poo without a jumbo is completely irr-elephant!'

The End

Author's note 1 – No animals were harmed in the writing of this book but the author did fall off his scooter a few times.

Author's note 2 – Hands up if you sniffed the pages of this book in Chapter 4? Thinking the paper was made from elephants dung? Did you taste it? Go on, try it now.

About the author, Stuart Reid

Stuart Reid is 50 years old, going on 10.

Throughout his early life he was dedicated to being immature, having fun and getting into trouble. After scoring a goal in the playground Stuart was known to celebrate by kissing lollypop ladies.

He is allergic to ties; blaming them for stifling the blood flow to his imagination throughout his twenties and thirties. After turning up at the wrong college, Stuart was forced to spend the next 25 years being boring, professional and corporate. His fun-loving attitude was further suppressed by the weight of career responsibility, as a business manager in the retail and hospitality industries in the UK and Dubai.

Stuart is one of the busiest authors in Britain, performing daily at schools, libraries, book stores and festivals with his book event Reading Rocks! He has appeared at over 1,000 schools and has performed to over 250,000 children. In 2015 Stuart was invited to tour overseas, with visits to schools in Ireland, Dubai and Abu Dhabi, with Malaysia scheduled for 2016.

He has performed his energetic and exciting book readings at the Edinburgh Fringe Festival, has been featured on national television, radio and countless newspapers and magazines. He won the Forward National Literature Silver Seal in 2012 for his debut novel, Gorgeous George and the Giant Geriatric Generator and was recently presented with the Enterprise in Education Champion Award by Falkirk Council.

Stuart has been married for over twenty years. He has two children, a superman outfit and a spiky haircut.

About the illustrator, John Pender

John is 37 and currently lives in Grangemouth with his wife Angela and their young son, Lucas, aged 6.

Working from his offices in Glasgow, John has been a professional graphic designer and illustrator since he was 18 years old, contracted to create illustrations, artwork and digital logos for businesses around the world, along with a host of individual commissions of varying degrees.

Being a comic book lover since the age of 4, illustration is his true passion, doodling everything from the likes of Transformers, to Danger Mouse to Spider-man and Batman in pursuit of honing his skills over the years.

As well as cartoon and comic book art, John is also an accomplished digital artist, specialising in a more realistic form of art for this medium, and draws his inspiration from acclaimed names such as Charlie Adlard, famous for The Walking Dead graphic novels, Glenn Fabry from the Preacher series, as well as the renowned Dan Luvisi, Leinil Yu, Steve McNiven and Gary Frank.

John has been married to Angela for 7 years and he describes his wife as his 'source of inspiration, positivity and motivation for life.' John enjoys the relaxation and stress-relief that family life can bring.

Photography is another of John's pleasures, and has established a loyal and enthusiastic following on Instagram.

More Gorgeous George Books

Gorgeous George and the Giant Geriatric Generator
The first Gorgeous George Adventure
Bogies, Baddies, bagpipes and burps!
Farting, false teeth and fun!
Kindle: http://goo.gl/tXB7x4

Gorgeous George and the ZigZag Zit-faced Zombies
Sneezing, sniffing, snogging and snots. Zombies,
zebras and zits!

**Gorgeous George and the Unidentified Unsinkable
Underpants Part 1**
Pumping, plesiosaurs, porridge and pants! Monsters, mayhem
and muck!

**Gorgeous George and the Unidentified Unsinkable
Underpants Part 2**
Tension, tunnels, trouser trumpets and tears.
Plesiosaurs, porridge and pants!

www.stuart-reid.com

Writing Rules OK

Writing Rules OK is Stuart Reid's creative writing workshop dedicated to inspiring children, young people (and teachers) to become aware of their unique power as writers, narrators and creative thinkers!

Each of the five modules looks at the specific elements of creative writing and includes exercises, classroom tools and homework sheets. The modules cover Genre, Plotting, Characters, Openers and Descriptives and these workshops can be classroom based, in small groups or as one-to-one coaching.

Writing Rules OK provides children and young adults with a basic knowledge and understanding of creative writing, with an opportunity to develop their own storytelling talents. There are several exercises included with each module, based on levels of ability, and includes Fast Finisher Extension Tasks, so whether your children are complete beginners or already becoming budding authors there's an exercise or two in each module to stretch everyone.

And there's no limit to the number of pupils or classes that can use the sessions; once you've bought each module, you can use them as often as you like. Although generally aimed at pupils between the ages of 8 and 14 years, each module lasts approx 1 hour, consisting of approx 15 minutes of audio summary and positioning, along with text-based exercises and worksheets.

www.writingrulesok.com

For Gorgeous George T-Shirts, Cups, Bags,
Notepads, Phone/iPad Cases and MANY other
products, please visit

http://www.redbubble.com/people/coldbludd/

collections/405936-gorgeous-george

THANK YOU!